# THE BIRTHDAY PICTURE

*and other stories*

# "The Birthday Picture"

*and other stories*

Written by Caitlin M.S. Buxbaum

Illustrated by Briana Bloom

**Red Sweater Press**

Wasilla, Alaska

2021

*The Birthday Picture and Other Stories*

Written by Caitlin M.S. Buxbaum

Illustrated by Briana Bloom

Requests for permission to make copies of any part of the work should be submitted online at redsweaterpress.com/contact or mailed to the following address: Red Sweater Press, P.O. Box 870414, Wasilla, Alaska, 99687.

redsweaterpress.com

Library of Congress Control Number: 2021902906

Body text set in Calisto MT

Chapter headings set in Centaur

Page numbers set in Century Gothic

First Edition

ISBN-13: 978-1-7332677-8-6

*for Uncle Jeff*

# Contents

# Introduction

THESE STORIES are the results of an imagination at work over a span of 10 years, from 2010 to 2020. They will take you from Iceland to Italy, the Midwest to New England, the present day to the 1920s, and more times and places in between. They are dark, and sad, and strange, and sometimes humorous. Perspectives and verb tenses vary. In truth, not every story is likely to please every reader. But through all runs at least one common thread: an illustration of some inevitability, some expression of the human condition; this, to me, is at the heart of storytelling.

I was a fiction writer before I became a poet, though I have clearly been more generous with the publication of my poetry since starting Red Sweater Press. It is my hope that this collection will entertain readers as well as alert them to my intended versatility as both an author and a publisher. My goal is not for anyone to take away some great message from my work(s), but if some special understanding or new insight is gained in exploring these pages, all the better. Interpretation is better left to the consumer, and I intend to remain mostly silent in the face of questions like, "what does this mean?" or "what was that story about?"

However you may be coming to this book — as a friend, fan, family member, or stranger — I thank you, and I wish you the most enjoyment in reading *The Birthday Picture and Other Stories*.

- Caitlin M.S. Buxbaum

# The Birthday Picture

*and other stories*

# Gullfoss

ARLISS STOOD on a rocky precipice above the abyss, the gelid white falls roaring beside him. He took a deep breath and coughed, the frigid air irritating his lungs. The weather was unseasonably cold — barely above freezing, in mid-September — and in direct correlation, he believed, to the disastrous event of that afternoon.

*Reykjavik*, he recalled — difficult to spell, but "exotically romantic," his sister had said. The holiday had been her suggestion, a much needed "ice breaker," she said, for his stagnant relationship. Arliss and Kimmy had been together four and a half years, the last three months of which had been particularly dull. In June she had unkindly explained to him what a drain he had been on her life and that, if he had any mind to marry her, he ought to propose right then and there.

They were at a cocktail party in London, hosted by Kimmy's employer.

"Alright then," he had said, and walked out of the room.

It was dark now — the air colder and the thundering waterfall, Arliss imagined, quieter. Perhaps he had simply become accustomed to its voice.

Arliss took another deep breath and looked up at the stars. He was reminded of the diamond in his coat pocket, removed it, and studied it against the sky.

The morning after the party, Kimmy had begged Arliss not to leave her, saying she had been wrong to give him an ultimatum. But the apology did not repair the relationship, and the couple grew distant as the weeks wore on.

When Arliss announced that he had purchased tickets to

Iceland, Kimmy responded with angry practicalities:

"How could you be so *stupid*, Arliss, we could've *used* that money!"

"I can't just *leave*, Arliss, what about my *job*?"

But, gradually, the luxury of such a trip began to appeal to Kimmy, and her affection for Arliss soared as the day drew near.

Beside the waterfall, Arliss slipped and fell on his bottom, barely avoiding a long drop to the rocky pool below. His body had grown weary from standing, and he found himself grateful for the seat.

He looked at the diamond once more, then threw it into the gulf.

When the moment had come, with Kimmy looking out over the falls, the sun setting on her blonde hair, a powerful morbidity came over Arliss. He put a hand on Kimmy's shoulder, gaining her attention, and smiled. She smiled back. And then he pushed her.

She was too shocked, he imagined, to have screamed, and fell silently into the deep, narrow canyon.

The wind on the cliffs picked up and Arliss shuddered. He stood, blew on his hands, and shook them for warmth. Facing the cascading reality of his crime, he closed his eyes, and let the ground give way beneath him. Perhaps he did want to be with her, after all.

# Sunday

I WAS MARRIED, once. She was French. Her name was Inès, and I suppose I should have known that any woman whose name means "chaste" (especially if she's French) is destined to live ironically. Personally, I think Inès was hell-bent on destroying the image her parents gave her from the very beginning. Just look at her kiddie pictures. You'll find a lot of red lipstick and bent-over kissing poses.

Anyway, it was a Sunday afternoon and she was out on the veranda drinking coffee from a wine glass in her beige-and-white swimsuit. It was a bikini, of course, and depending on the time of year, her skin blended in with either the white or the beige half of her top, so it always looked like one of her breasts was showing. Her hair was pretty long at the time, and she always had it down in the summer, so the sun could turn it all blonde, "like les filles américaines." I've always liked brunettes, myself, and for the most part, she was, but even when she wasn't...

Well, as I said, she was French.

So of course, with my two years of high school French and mediocre looks — I know it probably sounds like I'm being modest, but I assure you I'm not — I really didn't stand a chance. But we did get married. Bought a house in Pomona, and a black French Bulldog — to remind her of home, I thought. She was offended. Eventually she warmed up to him though, and in the end, I think she probably loved that dog more than she ever loved me.

But I'm not bitter about it.

Seriously though — why *should* Inès have married me?

6

It might have been because we met on a yacht. I suppose the idea of being pampered by a rich American guy who did a triple-take every time he looked at her while she was wearing that camouflage bathing suit may have appealed to her, but in the end it's a mystery.

So I wasn't surprised that she ran off. I don't know where she went or with whom (although I imagine he had some douche-y name like Clark or Sebastian or Jean-Pierre), but I know I wasn't surprised. I was glad she took the dog. I just woke up one morning and I knew. She wasn't coming back. I got out of bed and took a tour of the house, seeing if I could smell her in the kitchen or the shower or the creases of the chaise longue, but whether I could or not I don't remember. I just went and sat on the veranda in my underwear. I got such a bad sunburn on my chest that when the skin peeled it tangled in my chest hair so that I looked like a really unhygienic, modern-day Esau. And I remember thinking, 'damn, this is literally injury to insult' (and then of course I remembered that it was the other way around, and somehow that just made everything worse).

But it was on that Sunday when I saw her stretched out on a lawn chair in her beige-and-white bikini reading some girly magazine with a bright pink headline that said "600 ways to enjoy sex with your partner" that I realized what a total fuck-up I was. Still am, I guess.

"Inès," I said.

"Oui," she said, without looking up.

"Do you love me?"

I had her attention — for a moment. Then she continued reading. "Eez Sunday, Spensergh," she said, pronouncing my name with a touch of that guttural accent at the end.

"So?"

She muttered something in French.

"What?"

She frowned at me. "People don't talk about love on Sunday. It eez God's day."

I stared at her. "Maybe you should teach me some more French."

She slapped the magazine shut and pushed herself up from the chair, all arms and legs.

"Where are you going?"

"Ze bedroom. Come," she said, gliding past me. The utter embodiment of grace — in the physical sense, at least.

We went to bed and had the worst sex we've probably ever had. That probably anybody ever had. We didn't talk on Monday, and Tuesday morning she was gone.

Most people would probably say that Monday is the worst day of the week, and that I've just proved it. But it's still Sunday that I hate the most. If we had had that conversation and that terrible sex on a Monday, we could have blamed it on be-

8

ing Monday. On anything, really. I would have been skipping work — it would have been romantic and spontaneous. But we did it on "God's day." It was like he designed a day on which Inès and I were destined to fuck each other to kingdom come and God Almighty would still come out on top. I don't know that Inès was ever religious, but what chance did I have? I was not her god. And it wasn't even because I was just an average guy. I was Spenser Staten, the yacht guy. The ticket, the bridge, the rope, getting man-handled and stepped on until she'd reached the other side. But to me there was no other side. No matter how I craned my neck I could only have knowledge about what was immediately above or below me.

It's clever, really. Calling Sunday rest. You let your guard down. You think you can be Jean-Pierre or Clark or Sebastian during the week and on Sunday no one will know that you're really Spenser Staten, the yacht guy. But the Alpha and Omega does. And he's fucking your French wife while you rest on the fact that you're Spenser the yacht guy. Well, I won't be resting anymore. I'll rest when I'm dead. Which, admittedly, could be soon, given all the blasphemy I've been spouting.

Ah well. Tomorrow's Sunday. Maybe I'll go sit on the veranda.

# Fulfillment

"WHERE'S MY CANNOLI?" a little voice behind me says.

I turn to see a young boy of maybe six, dirty blond hair falling about his eyes as his head swivels, searching for his missing treat. His sister stands smirking beside him, sticky fingers gripping the Italian sweet behind her back.

Their mother scolds them for being noisy as she tries to talk to the woman seated next to her.

"Some days they're little monsters, aren't they," says the woman, sipping a frothy latte. I wonder if she has children of her own.

The mother smiles tiredly, returning to her adult conversation. I watch the children, racing around the table next to me.

"Give it back, Nina!" the boy yells, having discovered his cannoli's captor.

The girl, a brighter blonde, maybe a year older, sticks her tongue out at the boy. She makes to take a bite out of her stolen goody, when a larger hand snatches it away.

"You already had one, Nina," the mother says. "Let Jesse have his."

I smile, then slip out of the way as another patron walks past me. I instinctively offer my excuses, though he doesn't hear me.

The women are talking again, the mother's back to her children. Jesse quietly munches on his prize, deserved, kicking his legs back and forth as he sits. Nina has resorted to making art, rubbing her nubs of crayon on the page of a coloring book.

I take a seat closer to them, observing the somewhat jerky

movements of childhood, creative and energetic efforts expended in their separate, haphazard ways.

I feel eyes on me, turn around to see a man looking my way. But it is not me he sees — it is the mother of these children, the faces of the boy and girl. I'm wondering who should feel more embarrassed at being caught — him, or I — when the woman turns around to check on her offspring. She is not concerned by what she sees, and I am glad. It has been so long since I have enjoyed the presence of youth, all too absent in my life — years, I think, since I have dared to be so near to it, this young vivacity, in a public place.

"I can't imagine what that must have been like," I hear the mother say, and for a moment I think she is talking to me, can read my thoughts, even. It is only when I look up and see the other woman's face, daring to crumple with the weight of loss from long ago — distant, yet permanently painful — that I realize my mistake.

Miraculously, she manages a smile, gazes at Nina and Jesse. "I thought it broke me," she says, "but it only cracked my

shell. Expanded my capacity for love, Richard says, as I filled in the gaps."

"How?" the mother of Nina and Jesse asks, uncomprehending. "How did you fill them?"

The lonely woman, tall and dark, looks at the children again, now coloring in a jungle scene, together. I feel strangely protective of them, wanting to tell her they do not belong to her. But they do not belong to me either, and I am sad for the both of us.

Another customer comes by and nearly sits on me before I am able to move away. As I stand, I see Jesse and Nina's mother smile on her children.

"Jesse and Nina?" she asks her friend, surprise — and maybe fear, I imagine — coloring her voice.

The wistful smile of the tall dark woman disappears in shame, I think, as the distracted mother faces her again.

"Through all children, I suppose," she answers in a low voice. "They give me life."

Her eyes are full of tears as they rise to meet the other mother's.

"Oh Leah," is the consolation, with the squeeze of a hand. "I'm so glad."

The implication, I note, which Leah accepts, is that her friend is glad her children bring Leah joy, but that is not what I hear. I have been Leah, and I have met this other woman — the woman who thinks, "I'm so glad I'm not in your shoes."

I boil uncouthly with anger, wanting to scoop Jesse and Nina up for myself, to follow Leah home and drop them at her doorstep, say, "Take them. They're yours. You deserve them."

Of course, I cannot do any of this. Maybe I might have, had I known what I know now; had I met Leah in another life, and colluded with her to abduct love for the both of us.

But as the café fills, as this small party I have spied on gathers their things, more people pass by me and through me, reminding me of my place. I am a vapor. I have lived and died already, no longer capable of touch.

I drift out the door, steal one more unseen glance at these two children who have brought Leah so much joy, and whose mother cannot fully fathom the gift she has been given.

The women say their goodbyes, and while Nina hoists herself into her mother's vehicle, Jesse stops and stares — at me. I look behind and around me, but there is no one on the sidewalk, save us.

I stare back. I smile, and he smiles, then climbs into the car next to his sister. I wave as they drive past, but Jesse is already occupied by another facet of his reality, and I wonder if he actually saw me at all.

My eyes fall on Leah now, sitting in her car, weeping with memory. I slip into the seat next to her, whisper in her ear, "You are loved. You are special. You are known."

Her chin rises, and she blinks away the tears. As her head turns about, searching for my voice, I am pulled from the scene, into the black... the white...

The end.

# Coming Home

MAURA SANDERS was lying in a hospital bed waiting to die. At 24, she couldn't imagine a more terrible fate, but if she were honest with herself, she couldn't really imagine a better one, either. Maura was half Japanese, and if the American side of her died, so did her mother's heritage — maybe then, Reginald could finally let go of his regret over making such a family.

After all, "comfort women" were never meant to be mothers.

But Reginald loved Ayame, and Maura didn't have the heart to have him committed for his PTSD. Not that Ayame would have let her. He only hit Ayame a few times, after she'd cut her hair so short that she reminded him of a certain Japanese soldier he'd killed — whom he thought had come back to haunt him — but when it grew out again, he only yelled sometimes, when shootings were on the news. Still, Maura had tried to reason with her mother.

"He's not getting better, Mama," she'd said, several years ago, while her father was asleep.

Ayame had thrown her dishrag on the kitchen counter. "So? You don't put him in that place! Memory never go away — you can't take that from him!"

Maura heard her mother's double meaning: sending Reginald away wouldn't fix the problem, but even if he were able to forget the war, he would forget Ayame with it. But maybe, Maura thought, Ayame's love could heal him if they had more time to themselves. So she left.

It had occurred to Maura, at first, that she could just make herself more scarce at home, but that was no way to live; she was twenty years old, and she couldn't be so much of a burden as to come and go as she pleased, reminding them at any moment that their love had cost them their freedom and imposed on them a responsibility. Before Maura moved out, she wrote,

*I'm not leaving you my address, because I want you to act as though I am dead. No — as if I were never born. This way, you two can have whatever life you want, wherever love takes you. Do not try to find me.*

FOUR YEARS LATER, Maura was living in a studio apartment in Dublin, Ohio working as a Japanese language tutor and piano teacher. It happened that one Friday, in June, a student noticed Maura was not herself.

"Did I play it wrong again?" the young boy asked dejectedly, letting his hands fall into his lap.

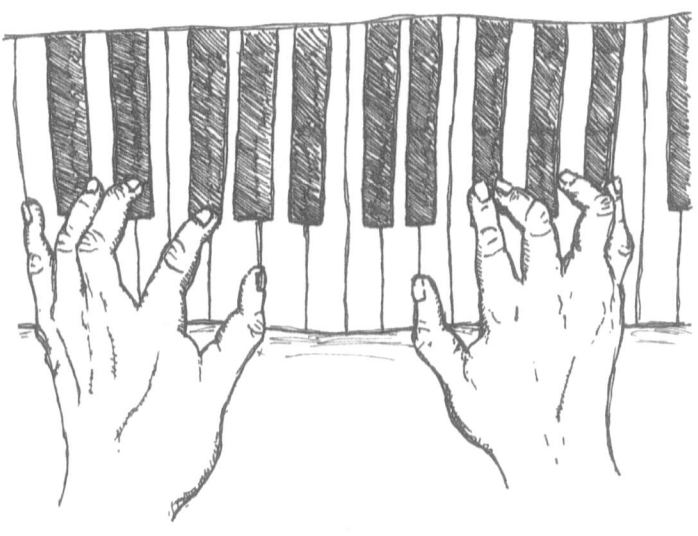

"No no Addie, you're really getting much better," Maura said, gripping the piano bench. She tried to sound consoling but the pinched expression on her face didn't have the boy convinced. Maura's stomach flipped and she sprinted to the bathroom, miraculously making it to the toilet before vomiting violently. Maura stared into the bowl, waiting for her vision to clear, but the color never changed: blood red.

"*Sensei?*" Addie asked timidly from the doorway. "Are you sick?"

After a long moment, Maura said hoarsely, "You can go home early today, Addie. Tell your mom we'll pick up next week. You can use the phone in the kitchen."

Maura waited until she heard the boy's little feet padding away to get up, and, confirming that the nausea had subsided, flushed the toilet, washed her hands, and brushed her teeth. She hoped Mrs. Larsen wouldn't see fit to hire a new teacher; with the rate Addie and his sister were learning, Maura wouldn't be surprised if a little illness put her out of a job.

In the next week, she vomited blood five times, and three doctor visits later, a gray-haired man in a white coat gave her the diagnosis: stomach cancer. It was mid-July when Maura arrived at the cancer hospital in Zion, Illinois to have the tumor removed, but after surgery, a small piece remained, and the tumor began to grow again.

"This is really very uncommon," the young surgeon said, his face red as he fidgeted with the clipboard in his hands. "I realize... that is, we'll have to give you some more time to recover, but we'd like to operate one more time once you're... when that's happened."

Maura stared out the window as a cloud moved in front of the sun. The surgeon rubbed his neck. "If you don't... that is, if you would like me to... I'll come back when you're feeling better," he ended hastily, hurrying out of the room. Maura scoffed at the probability of her "feeling better" any time soon.

She watched the clouds drift for a while before she drifted off to sleep herself.

IN THE MORNING, the red-faced surgeon returned with more of the same forms from before for Maura to sign, and he was met with more silence.

"Is there anyone we can call that might help you with any preparations you might need to make?" the surgeon asked, innocently enough, but Maura would have none of it.

"Preparations?!" she shouted, snapping up into a sitting position. "For idiot doctors' mistakes?! TO HELL WITH YOU!" Maura shrieked, throwing a vase from the bedside table at the man's head. The glass shattered against the wall to his left and he sped out of the room, white as a sheet. After that, it was an older doctor that visited Maura with similar speeches and questions, but after six different doctors and the same number of broken, throwable objects, they finally stopped pushing consent forms at her. Puzzled, but legally bound, they put her in a small, pale blue room in the back of the cancer ward. Days turned into weeks, and still the tumor grew, however slowly. Whatever pain it caused her, Maura showed no sign of any discomfort, nor any other emotion. Unlike the tantrums she had thrown before, it was now her bizarre stoicism that spread around the hospital as Maura's distinguishing characteristic. That, and her Japanese mumbling from time to time — *unsan musho* — which the hospital employees could only translate as "scattered clouds, disappearing mist."

IT WAS THE LAST DAY of July and rain had been lightly pelting her window all day. Though she couldn't see through the closed blinds, Maura imagined huge purple clouds weighing down the sky. As she lay listening to the weather, the door opened without a knock of courtesy. She considered feigning sleep, but curiosity got the better of her. She opened her eyes and turned

17

her head to see the back of a small, sandy-haired boy as he quietly closed the door.

"Oh," he said, finding Maura watching him. "You're awake." The boy smiled and made his way over to the bed. Maura continued to stare at him in confusion, but he seemed to be waiting for her to speak.

"And who might you be?" she finally asked.

The boy's smile whitened with the showing of his perfect teeth. Maura looked at him blankly.

"I'm Addie," the boy said, crossing the floor to her bedside.

*Of course*, Maura thought, wondering how she hadn't recognized him sooner. Yet, in a way, he looked older, as if he had not grown in size, but was a man of miniature proportions. As she stared at him in wonder, another presence arrived in the room.

"His given name is Adelard," said a bitter voice from the doorway. A somber-looking girl with wide-set eyes glared at Maura. *Mia*.

Addie frowned at his sister, and Maura found herself surprised at the displeasure it gave her to see his cherubic face so distorted. "I thought you were going to wait with Mother, Mia," he said.

The girl hesitated and glanced at Maura, who was observing the lank, dirty blonde hair that fell down to her flat chest. Mia wore a knee-length, pale blue dress that her fair skin almost matched. Maura imagined that the girl might have disappeared into the wallpaper had she leaned against it, and an odd giggle escaped her lips. Mia looked at her strangely, and a shadow fell over Maura's face. She did not want to be judged by this teenage girl with the "be careful, she's crazy" expression on her face.

Crazy. Mentally unstable. *Dangerous*. All of these words came to Maura's mind, and she wondered which one applied to her, but it was only the last description that gave her a little thrill. *Dangerous.*

Mia's unusually cold voice brought Maura back to the scene before her.

"She went to the restroom, and she told me to come find you," Mia answered. "She says we're leaving soon."

Adelard turned back to Maura, and to her inexplicable relief, he was smiling again. "I suppose I ought to get straight to the point then."

Maura almost laughed at the boy's formality, then thought better of it, suddenly desperate to hide her questionable mental state from him. She waited patiently for him to continue, keeping an eye on his freakishly tall sister.

Addie laid a tiny hand on Maura's smooth, olive arm. She inhaled sharply, in awe of the sensation — it was as if his skin were a part of her own. Maura shot a furtive look at Mia to see if she had noticed the change, but she was only looking at Maura blankly. Maura gazed into Addie's shining blue eyes, searching for answers.

"Why are you here?" she whispered.

"To give you a message," the boy breathed.

"And what about you?" Maura asked Mia loudly, as if to challenge the girl to break the strange new bond between her and Addie.

Mia hesitated, then took a step forward and stopped awkwardly between Maura and the door. "I heard the message too," she said quietly.

"And?" Maura asked the boy, suddenly anxious. She set her left hand gently on top of his, and he grinned. Mia's face softened and the atmosphere seemed calmer. Still, Maura awaited the answer to her query with bated breath.

Addie's smile flattened. He licked his lips, pink and cracked.

"Your mother," he began gently, then paused for a long time. A range of emotions sped through Maura, without it showing on her face. She waited.

Finally, Adelard began again. "We were there when she died." Shock jolted through Maura as she tried to understand the meaning of his words. Had her mother really died? When?

"How did she die?" Maura asked, trembling.

For a second, Mia didn't hear her because she spoke so quietly. As understanding hit, she gasped and glared at Addie.

"I told you to find out if someone had told her first!" Mia scolded, quickly crossing the room to tower over her brother. Addie's ensuing grimace was so heartbreaking to Maura that, for a moment, she forgot her own pain, and sat up to touch the boy's cheek. They stayed like that for a moment before Mia straightened up and folded her arms, then took the liberty of answering Maura's question:

"It was about a year ago. We were visiting our grand-mother's grave by the beach when we saw someone walking up the path to the cliffs, and we decided to follow her." Mia paused and bit her lip, staring at her feet. "When she reached the top, we weren't far behind her, and she heard us. She was standing at the edge of the cliff and... and she said..."

The girl stopped again, as if she were afraid to finish. No, it wasn't so much fear, Maura thought; it was that uncertainty again, whether or not Mia could trust Maura's mental state. Maura watched the girl's eyebrows crease in what would have been a comical way, but for the circumstances; Maura let the laughter die inside her, and Addie spoke again.

"It was something in Japanese, I think. I might say it wrong, but... I think she said, 'Ma-chan... ie ni kite kudasai. Anata... watashi no kokoro desu.'"

Silent, soft tears began to pool beneath Maura's closed eye-lids, some spilling out onto her cheeks as she heard the words in her mother's voice.

"Please," Addie pled quietly, his own eyes turning glassy. "The words. What do they mean?"

*Maura dear... please come home. You are my heart, my mind,* Maura translated in her head, but she couldn't speak the words.

Her eyes snapped open. "Addie. Adelard. *Sono ato nani ga...* What happened after that?" Maura asked in a fierce whisper, slipping into Japanese in her haste. The boy looked up at her, his eyes wide with... what it was, Maura could not place. Seized with something like despair, she grabbed hold of the boy's shoulders and shook him.

"*NANIGA OKOTTANOKA*? TELL ME!" Maura's shrill voice was riddled with sobs. Tears rolled down Addie's cheeks, but he made no movement in his crying.

"She fell," Mia murmured vaguely. She did not look at Maura when she pulled Adelard away from her grasp and gathered him to her thin body. His satiny hair clung to the spot on her chest where a grown woman's bosom would be, but instead there appeared to be a wall. Maura leaned back and let her arms fall where they would. She closed her eyes in defeat and continued to weep for a long time. She hadn't meant to startle the boy or anger the girl — for whatever reason she could possibly be angry — but it had been so long since Maura had shown any emotion, felt anything so strong as what her mother had allegedly felt for her in her final moments. And she had spoken in Japanese, reaching out to that part of Maura that had always screamed of shame to her — if not for Japan, would her father have had to go to war? But he would not have met Ayame. *Watashi no kokoro*, she had called her. *My heart. My mind. My core.*

But in the grief, in the waves of confused emotion that continued to wash over Maura as she silently begged her mother to explain why, then, did she leave Maura alone, her heart began to swell. Ayame Ito had taken what was left of her life

when Maura — Ayame's soul — had chosen to die. But Maura would revive Ayame's *kokoro*. She would show her mother she had not truly died. She would choose to live.

A GENTLE TAPPING woke Maura from her dream. "Miss Sanders, I have a letter for you! Oh, but it's so dark in here!"

Maura opened her eyes to see a short, squat woman with bushy red hair pudder over to the window and release the shade. Maura shut her eyes quickly, then smiled with the warmth from the sun. The nurse returned to her patient and set the letter on the bedside table. Unaware that Maura was indeed awake, she stared curiously into her tear-stained, faintly smiling face for a moment, then made for the door again in silence.

"Did anyone come in to visit me?" Maura asked in a hurried voice, just as the woman reached for the door handle. She jumped in surprise, then smiled at Maura sympathetically.

"No, not yet I'm afraid."

Maura thought she should frown, but she could only feel bliss — and resolve.

"Well, could you send for the doctor? I'd like to sign the consent form."

The nurse stared at Maura for a moment before understanding slowly registered on her face. "Oh! Oh of course, just let me..."

The nurse moved to leave again, then paused halfway out the door, turning back to Maura. "Excuse me, but... what made you change your mind?"

Maura sat for a moment in silent contemplation. "A message," she answered, with a far-off look in her eyes.

Getting the feeling that she ought not to press further, lest Maura change her mind again, the nurse hurried out the door and tapped down the hallway to the doctor's office as fast as her pudgy little legs could carry her.

Maura sat up and wiped the tears from her face, then picked the letter up off the table. It was a piece of expensive-looking stationery, folded in thirds, unsealed. She unfolded the letter and read the few short lines written in an unfamiliar, elegant script:

*Dear Miss Sanders,*

*I hope you are not bothered by my intrusion, but my husband is on business in Chicago and my children begged to visit you. One of the nurses said you were asleep, and we were on a bit of a time crunch, so I told them to write you a note instead, and Addie wanted to draw you a picture. Mia has also written you a poem — I hope this brings as much comfort to you as it did to them in making it. Get well soon.*

Below these four sentences was a crayon drawing of a small boy holding hands with a dark-haired, light-olive-skinned woman, who held hands with a tall girl on her other side. They seemed to be on a beach, with a giant blue sea stretching out behind them, a big yellow sun directly overhead, and little black Vs for birds on the horizon. Next to the drawing of the girl was written, in a steadier hand,

*By the sea, in heart and mind*
*The salty sea flows behind*
*Like days reaching into light*
*Staying the terrors of the night·*

At the bottom of the page were three signatures: Addie, Amy Larsen, and Mia. Maura put a hand to her mouth and held the letter to her chest, letting tears slide out from beneath her lashes again.

There was a knock at the door and the young, red-faced surgeon strode swiftly into the room, apparently having regained some confidence in the last month or so. Briefly measuring Maura's current state, and being satisfied, he muttered some pleasantries and handed her a clipboard and a pen. He then began to softly state the risks of the procedure, as fast as he could, and watched with shining eyes as the pen tip glided across the bottom of the page. Maura handed him back the clipboard with a small smile, which he returned with a grin.

"Congratulations, Miss Sanders. In a matter of days, you'll be cured. You'll be able to go home," the doctor said.

Maura's lips held their smile as she turned to look out the window, watching the clouds part for the sun outside.

"Yes," she said serenely. "Home." The doctor gave Maura a quick nod and moved to the door, but Maura stopped him.

24

"Could you do me a favor?" she asked politely. The doctor gazed at her warily, and Maura felt a brief pang of guilt for terrifying him so. "It's just... I'd like to you to call my parents, is all. Let them know I'm here."

The doctor's eyes widened in surprise, but he refrained from commenting and passed her the clipboard again. She scribbled the number in the corner and smiled, handing it back to him. He looked at the number briefly, glanced at Maura, and left the room without another word.

Maura let her eyes be drawn back to the pale blue wallpaper, imagining Mia fading in and out of it, then back to the window where Addie's blond head came out of the sun. Maura looked back and forth between the two visions for a long time. *Watashi no kokoro...*

FIVE DAYS LATER, Maura Sanders was in the recovery wing, tumor free.

"How d'you feel?" the doctor asked brightly, but Maura wasn't listening. As he talked, she watched a short Asian woman get out of her car through the hospital window. A tan, graying man got out of the passenger side slowly.

"We'll have to monitor you for a few more days, of course, just to make sure everything's in order, all ship-shape and whatnot, no bleeding or anything, and then you'll be outta here. Just don't forget to write," the doctor said chuckling.

Although Maura didn't quite know where "out of here" would lead, she found herself smiling.

"*Okaasan,*" she whispered to the couple walking into the hospital, arm in arm. "Papa. *Ie ni kimasu.*"

*Mother, Papa. I am coming home.*

# In Bloom

It was that first night in August when Lily Böhn tip-toed across the cobbles of Isola Bella to the pier in her pink ballet slippers that she heard the gospel truth from Harvey Whittaker. Wearing a pair of dusty khaki shorts and a bright red tie with his grubby, brown corduroy blazer unraveling at the cuffs, Harvey sat slumped over an empty bowl of clam chowder, his hairy legs dangling over the side of the pier. The graying curls on his head were mussed on one side as if he had been sleeping for days, as still as the stones beneath his 68-year-old bottom. The scruff on his sun-tanned jowls and neck made him look just as disheveled, but his eyes said otherwise. Wooden in color yet very much alert with consciousness, his irises seemed to simultaneously reach deep into some sweet and philosophical spot in a dark corner of his mind, and out to the silently exploding colors on the horizon beyond the Borromean Gulf. An almost visibly salty sea breeze snatched away the remnants of the stifling humidity from the afternoon, causing Harvey's eyelids to close as his chapped lips parted in a toothy smile.

It was in this state that Lily's virgin feet came to rest gracefully behind him, under the shade of a cypress tree. The little yellow barrette pinning back Lily's fair hair stuck out at such an angle, one might have expected it to jump right into Harvey's lap. Still, the lips of both girl and clip stayed latched as Harvey spoke.

"Sky's cloudin' up suh'm beautiful t'night," he murmured wistfully, imbibing the lingering dregs of light and warmth from the sun. The star of the scene was now setting in a ring of silk-drawn clouds like the eye of a celestial storm. "Is just about time."

"Time for what?" Lily asked without moving, her voice just far enough above a whisper to be carried to the end of the pier.

"Oh, y'know. Dinner, fer some. Dusk. Th'end of happy hour. Limbo, I s'pose."

"What?"

"Limbo — y'know what—"

"I know what limbo is. What I meant was, I don't understand."

Lily moved out of the shadows and sat at the northern edge of the pier, removing her shoes as she spoke.

"Don' unnerstand what? If y'knows what limbo is, what's else to make sense?"

"Well it's *after* dinner for me, it isn't even *close* to dusk, and I don't see any reason why happiness can only last an hour, or what limbo has to do with any of it." She stated these things more as fact than explanation, touching her toes to her own little corner of the sea with their 13 years of wisdom and wear.

"H'ain't that the truth!" Harvey boomed, shaking into coarse laughter with a slap on his puddle of a knee. He set the empty bowl on his left, then turned over his right shoulder to survey his company. The knotty muscles in his face contracted and his mustache quivered as he realized Lily's age. "Now, whatsa child like you doin' out here so late?"

"I could ask you the same question," Lily replied, sweeping the blonde curtain between Harvey and herself behind her ear. Rather than meeting his gaze, she continued to look just north of the fiery glow receding behind the knoll across the bay, where the clouds had cleared and indigo was being gathered to the earth in a shower of stars.

"Well I s'pose you could, but it wu'n't make much sense since I'm no child!"

"Aren't you?" This time Lily delivered her response with a curious stare from her gray-blue eyes.

Harvey raised his eyebrows. "Well shoot, I guess I am. Not in the way you might've heard though, I'd bet."

Lily continued to stare, but Harvey had turned his back on her and resumed the same paradoxically introspective and outward-reaching expression as before. After pulling her feet out of the water and back onto the pier, Lily gathered the skirt of her lilac dress and stood up. Abandoning her slippers, she painted watery footprints all the way up to where Harvey sat and waited to find the invisible pair of glasses through which he saw the setting sun. Harvey looked up and scooted over to make a spot for the girl, which she quietly accepted. The two of them looked at each other's knees, one pair white and nubile, the other dark and arthritic, riddled with traces of varicose veins.

Harvey chuckled. "These bones don' look too young

though, do they?" He turned to Lily as he asked the question, but she was squinting out into the ocean again, still trying to see through Harvey-colored lenses.

"Aunt Rhee says you haven't been back to America in years."

Harvey's lips peeled back in a smile. "Oh, well that's true enough. I don' suppose your Aunt Rhee's been back there much 'erself if she been around here long enough to know that."

"No, she went to see my sister in California last summer," Lily said, missing the deeper meaning in Harvey's words. "She said twenty-one was a good age for Ally to bond with her."

"Ho-ho, well I bet!" Harvey's rough laughter coursed through the air again. "If 'bondin'' means shootin' the breeze with a bottle-a rum!"

Lily frowned. "Ally doesn't drink that much. She didn't even wanna drink when she turned twenty-one, but Aunt Rhee said it's always good for a special occasion."

"No, I s'pose your aunt and sister'd be more the type for a bottle-a Madeira in any case," Harvey said, ignoring the bulk of Lily's defense. "But don't you go gettin' any ideas now missy."

"Lily," she interjected.

"Whussat now?"

"My name's Lily."

"Oh, right then, nice to meet you miss Lily. I'm Harvey," the old man replied, extending his hairy hand.

"I know." Lily let her delicate white fingers be engulfed by his, twice as fat and not as long as hers.

"Well, alright then!" Harvey exclaimed. Pretending to be offended, he added, "I bet your aunt ain't told you everthin' about me, and she don' know the half of it neither!"

"She says you're the homeless island hermit." An impish

smirk grew on Lily's face. She was goading him now, challenging him to contradict her.

"Ha!" Harvey barked, still in good humor. "I s'pose that's true enough too."

Lily was slightly disappointed he hadn't taken her bait, allowed them to be equals in the bickering of good friends. Then again, there were hardly any similarities that she could see between an old, homeless hermit bumming around Italy and an American teenager fated to live with her aunt for the next five years. Lily liked Italy well enough, but Aunt Rhee was not cut out for raising a two-year-old on her own, much less keeping track of Lily.

Her eyes were positively straining now in the brilliant red light resting on the sea, right at eye level. Lily thought of her sister Ally's sultry red lipstick and wondered why she had not personally raided her aunt's supply already...

"But what was I sayin' agin?" Harvey broke into Lily's daydream of what it would feel like to press the waxy paint to her lips. "Before you introduced yourself."

The sun returned to its typical shape in Lily's eyes, no longer resembling Ally's ruby lips. "That I shouldn't get any ideas," she answered.

"Well that was rather dumb of me, wa'n't it? You get all the ideas you want now, Lily, just take a page out of your sister's book and go easy on the juice. 'Course you're 'llowed to have fun once in a while, when you're young, but don' go gettin' sloshy every Tuesdee."

"Sloshy?"

"Oh nevermind," Harvey said hastily. "Ignorance is bliss, eh? Or maybe naivete."

Lily frowned. "Aunt Rhee says that's not a good saying."

"Well why—how old is your Aunt Rhee?"

"Thirty-two."

"Ah," Harvey said knowingly, placing his hands on the pier behind him. "Not too old, not young enough neither, I'd say. She probably feels more strongly about the second part though, eh?"

"I don't know," Lily said. "She's old enough to be a mom." Gita's fragile face appeared in Lily's mind. She hoped Aunt Rhee remembered to put her to bed soon...

"Well, havin' a baby won' make you a grown-up but raisin' one will!" Harvey coughed another chuckle and continued: "Growin' up's not the hard part though is it, stayin' young's the trick."

"Aunt Rhee says she did."

"Did what?"

"Had a hard time growing up. Her parents got divorced when she was nine and Uncle Marlo — her brother — left when she was my age."

"Is that right? Well—and what *is* your age?"

"Thirteen." She tried to hide the annoyance in her voice at revealing such a signifying trait; age, in her experience, often had the power to change an adult conversation into something much more trivial in an insignificant amount of time.

Harvey whistled. "And your Aunt Rhee lets you out here so late?"

Lily shrugged, that curtain of hair falling between them again. "It's fine," she said.

"Hmm," Harvey mused, unconvinced. He tilted his heavy head back and eyed Lily skeptically, then found her face contorted in a contemplative grimace.

"Why the long face?"

Lily turned in his direction without looking him in the eye. "What you said about growing up," she answered. "Ally doesn't want to pay bills and stuff like that like Aunt Rhee has to, but she doesn't have any problem staying young. She always tells me to be a kid but I don't see what's so bad about twenty-one, or sixteen, or thirty-two…"

"Ho-ho, well you've got a while before that!" Harvey broke in. "Your sister's right though, about not rushin' things, but all that logistical stuff will come easily enough. She'll be jus' fine." Harvey leaned forward again and rested the palms of his hands on his knees. His arms were a bit short to meet them comfortably, however, so he pulled back a little and scratched at a stain on his pant leg. The dark blue blanket in the north had crept closer to the horizon, and the air was no longer warm enough to tempt teenagers into swimming. Lily waited for Harvey to say more, but when he finally spoke, the words were not what she expected.

"Lily."

Her face looked paler now in the dimming light, soaking up more "cold" colors than warm. "Yeah?"

"What's your middle name?"

Lily resisted the urge to raise her eyebrows; she wanted to see where he was going without distracting him. "Anne."

"Lily Anne." Harvey put a hand on her arm and pushed that mysterious corner of his mind out a little further from his eyes. "Lily Anne, I want you to remember something. When your sister Ally or your Aunt Rhee tells you to act like a grown-up or stop behavin' like a child, you remember that the only thing wrong with that, being a child, is embarrassing society, and society duh'n't know you like Ally or Aunt Rhee, and nobody knows you like you do."

Lily opened her mouth to form a response, but nothing came to mind. She shut it, looked back and forth between Harvey's eyes, searching for the crime society said he committed.

"Okay," she answered.

Satisfied, Harvey lifted his hand from her arm and replaced it on his thigh, returning his gaze to the last purple lip of the sun's light flowering into dusk.

"Well, I maybe misspoke earlier, but it's gettin' on dusk now and I bet your Aunt Rhee would like it better if you were home with her."

Lily sighed and stood up, careful not to be unladylike with the flipping of her skirt. "Oh, she doesn't mind. Little Gita gives her enough trouble, and she's only two."

Harvey opened his mouth to comment but Lily interrupted him. "Anyway, it was nice to meet you mister... well, what's your last name?"

"Oh we don' need to be botherin' with all that," Harvey said with a shooing motion of his hand. "But m'daddy's name was Whittaker, Mama's name was Pearson, granddaddies were Anton an' Quentin, so I'm Harvey Anton Pearson Quentin Whittaker."

Lily smiled. "All right, Harvey. Nice to meet you."

"And you as well, Lily Anne."

Lily padded back to pick up her slippers on the quickly cooling cement, then hesitated. Harvey's back was hunched and facing her, in the same position she had found him. She thought of calling out to him, racking her brain for some acceptable means of offering him a place to sleep. Finding none, she turned her back on him as well, and retreated past the cypress tree and away from Isola Bella.

The walk to Aunt Rhee's was short with Harvey's words still in her mind to accompany her, and soon the little Italian flat greeted her with a warm bed and a view of the stars that transported her into dreams of fire, flowers, and feet, on a cobblestone pier by the sea.

# Limbo

THE ROD OF THE POOL CUE glided back and forth between Martin's slim fingers as he surveyed the field before him: the odds were not in his favor. Three balls remained — one striped, one solid, and the eight ball, right in front of the left corner pocket. Number five sat pulsating in its flamboyant orange just to the left and two inches in front of the Black Magic, actively reminding Martin of the pressure he was under: "I'm the last one!" it seemed to exclaim. "You have to pocket me!" Still, the situation screamed impossibility.

Martin exhaled loudly and settled into position from the right side of the table to knock the cue ball hard and fast, as close to the left edge of number five as he could make it — it was his only hope.

Jonas watched from the shadows behind the same pocket the eight-ball guarded, his head and shoulders silhouetted by the glow of a neon pink flamingo sign. It was hard to see in the dim light of the bar just how dirty his white undershirt was, or how menacing he looked in the brown bomber jacket he always wore. To Martin's knowledge, no one had ever seen him without it, and for some reason, this was a comfort to him — although it was ominous not to know what lay underneath, he was glad not to have a concept of the raw power that could, no doubt, be summoned if the jacket came off. It was just better not to know, he reasoned, what fate he might meet in such a case. Still, Martin was under no illusion that he would or could actually win, and if that was the case, what could there be to worry about?

And yet, he really wanted to win.

Martin pulled back slowly on the pool cue one last time,

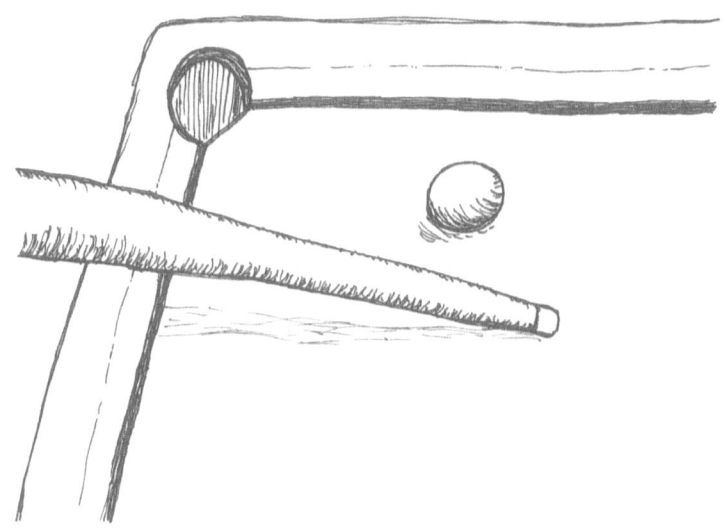

homed in on number five and slammed the chalky tip into the cream of the cue ball. A miniature cloud of blue smoke puffed into the air before the rolling ivory orb, creating the image of a strange, enormous white eye with a hazy blue iris and no pupil.

Rolling.

Searching.

Probing.

Martin was suddenly aware that he was no longer watching the movement of the billiard balls, but staring straight into the eyes of a man who now seemed much more — or less, depending on how you looked at it — than that. Jonas's gaze did more than pierce Martin with its direct intensity; it ripped into him with a bestial voracity that only increased when Jonas bared his teeth in a devilish grin.

The cue ball tapped the solid flame of number five, causing it to kiss the soulless black of number eight. A dull thunk resounded in the corner pocket, and the significance of the sound filled the room. The game was over. Martin became completely unhinged.

"You—you—he's a cheat!" Martin screeched, wrenching himself from the cruel blue eyes in the shadows to address the other patrons. The last word was so high-pitched that it was almost lost on the audience, but he had their attention. "The ball—he—he's a wizard, or a fucking hypnotist, did you see? Did you see?!"

The men seated at the counter swiveled back to the bar and hunched over their beers, not wanting to get involved. Whatever Jonas was, no one wanted to make eye contact with him or the crazed man appealing to anyone who would look his direction.

"I had it! The five! The eight was—it was—i-i-it shouldn't have—I could have made it!" Martin was in hysterics at the injustice of it all. It hardly mattered whether he won or lost — he was grateful not to invoke the resultant wrath of winning — but it was downright bad sportsmanship to cheat, he told himself.

The bartender set the pint glass he had been cleaning back on the shelf behind him and threw the rag into the sink. He cautiously made his way around to the other side of the bar and tried to talk some sense into the grown man turning into a blubbering block of gelatin before him.

"Now c'mon Marty, is jest a game, you know Jonas never—"

"DON'T CALL ME MARTY!" Martin screeched again, straining his vocal chords so much that he began to cough violently. Someone handed him a glass of water and he began taking huge gulps before he thought to identify his savior. Jonas had moved from beneath the flamingo to replace the billiard balls in their triangle, half-illuminated by the shaft of light trickling in the high, dirty window of the pub. Martin cast a furtive look toward the movement and suddenly spat out his mouthful of water, dropping the glass as well.

"Jesus, Marty, now who's gonna clean that up?" the bartender asked irritably, gesturing toward the shattered glass.

"POISON!" Martin screamed, ignoring both the hated nickname and the question. He stared at Jonas, breathing heavily, but addressed the bartender: "What in the hell kind of joint are you running?!"

"Now Martin, I—"

Jonas was suddenly towering over Martin, breathing the scent of sweet tobacco into his face. "That's all right, Cal. He doesn't mean any disrespect to you, I'm sure, but I'm curious to know why Martin believes I poisoned him."

Martin's knees threatened to buckle at the nearness of his opponent, but his feet were rooted to the spot, just as his eyes were to Jonas's cold expression. The two-day-old scruff on his neck and face hid the pockmarks of innumerable scars, and even though Martin was blind to them, he was scared stiff, utterly lost for words.

"Well?" Jonas asked, as calmly as before.

Martin tried to communicate: "I—I-I-I—"

"That's enough of the stuttering, I think." Jonas laid a hand over Martin's mouth to silence him, and the littler man's eyes grew wide. Before another word left Jonas's lips, Martin's eyes rolled back, and he collapsed on the beer-stained floor.

No one moved.

Jonas scanned the room for witnesses, searching for any shocked expressions, but he found none. Cal continued to look at the ground and shuffle his feet uncomfortably under Jonas's mystifying stare.

"I suppose you ought to call the authorities there, Cal. I suspect Martin may need some medical assistance."

Cal shivered at his calm, calculated tone, and mumbled something like, "sure, s'right, oughta call somebody," retreating to the phone behind the counter to carry out Jonas's instructions. He punched in 911 and began muttering into the receiver, noticing the pub quickly emptying as wary customers slipped out the front door. To the remaining three or four patrons skulking in the corners, too ashamed to show their drunken faces in public so early in the evening, Jonas voiced his farewell:

"Enjoy the rest of your evening, gentlemen." Chuckling at the lack of response, he turned his back on the lounge and spat on the floor just behind the pool table. The bartender hung up the phone and hurried back around the counter to clean up the broken glass, careful not to get in Jonas's way. Before disappearing into the dark and out the back door, Jonas rapped his knuckles on a wooden support beam at the end of the counter. In that second, Cal could just make out the six letters tattooed on the back of his right hand: SINNER. Cal's blood ran cold, but Jonas was already gone.

# For All We Know

WHEN KENNY SHOT CHARLIE, no one was really sure how to react. It wasn't because it was all that surprising — Kenny had had it out for Charlie since day one — but we didn't know whether to rejoice at the end of the feud or dread whatever was coming next.

The bullet hit Charlie in the chest, right beneath the collarbone, on the wrong side. That is, if Kenny had been trying to kill him, anyone would've thought he'd aim for the heart. Now there was no chance Kenny could've shot that poorly at a range of 10 feet, but no one could think of a good reason why he would've shot Charlie without intending to kill him. Charlie's a good four inches taller than Kenny, and noticeably burlier, too; we figured wounding a guy like that would be a lot like picking a fight with a grizzly bear, armed with nothing but a hot branding iron. It just didn't make any sense.

Charlie died less than two hours later, and we weren't any closer to figuring out why everything unfolded as it did (or what the proper response to the whole thing was) when Kenny showed up at the cop shop, stuck a gun in his mouth and shot himself right in front of the attendant. (Next day the papers said the desk jockey was no more than a 23-year-old kid, fresh on the job that week, who got scared shitless watching a stranger lose their staring contest by blowing his brains out.) We were downright stumped. The whole town was. Kenny was always quiet in school, a skinny blond kid with glasses and straight Cs through high school, except for a B-minus he got in shop class. But when Charlie came to town it was like a modern-day Wild West cowboy turf war settled in.

Charlie had a smile for everyone — most teachers loved

him, and a lot of students did, too (with the exception of Kenny), but he probably wasn't the *most* popular. He wasn't much for sports, except pick-up basketball, occasionally, and then he got kicked off the tennis team for taking a whiz right outside the court at a match. (He never bothered to appeal the ejection.) Other than that one offense, he was usually pretty polite and didn't try to get away with anything neither — he just seemed like a regular guy. But there was something about him that drove Kenny into such a rage whenever he laid eyes on big bear Charlie that anyone could see the steam coming out of his ears from a mile away.

Less than a week after the shootings, the papers printed some nonsense about Kenny being bullied as a child — just to confirm the clichés, I guess — but we all knew it had to be deeper than that. The kind of blind hatred Kenny had for Charlie didn't come from a slow buildup of swirlies and getting jumped for lunch money, and I'm sure it wasn't any of that cyberbullying garbage people are going on about these days.

Kenny's revulsion seemed unique in the fact that it stayed the same from when he first saw Charlie's face to the day they died. But none of us could believe he was just a psychopath, neither. He came from a good family out in the country with two younger siblings — a brother and a sister — with no family history of mental illness or disability. The only criminal record was his great uncle Thythik's from when he tried not to pay his taxes and ended up doing it anyway.

So where was the motive (for the hatred, not the murder)? What made Kenny Kilbourne "snap," the news reporters asked. Well, they got his 24-year-old sister Sandy to answer some questions on some prime-time TV program that puzzled people even more.

*TV interviewer: How would you describe your older brother, recently deceased?*

*Sandy Kilbourne: Dead.*

*TVI: [flustered] Well, yes, but ah...before that. As your brother, flesh and blood. ...?*

*Sandy picked at her long, unpolished fingernails in serious concentration for a few seconds, then smiled briefly at the camera and said, "Flesh and blood he may have been but my brother Kenny ain't really my brother Kenny. His ma adopted me after Charlie's ma — my ma — decided she didn't want me."*

Now, as you can imagine, her saying that raised all sorts of questions and quite a bit of scandal that both sets of parents was none too happy to have revealed on television after the deaths of their 30-year-old sons, but that was just the tip of the iceberg.

*Sandy tossed back her straight blonde hair with a flick of her head and flung her arms across the lap of her hot pink dress. "Kenny was more of a brother to me than Charlie was, but Charlie was so straight with me I couldn't hold it against him," she said seriously. "I handed him my phone number a*

41

*week after I met him, when I was a freshman in high school, and he looked me straight in the face with that sad smile of his and told me I was his sister without even looking at the note. I slapped him good and hard across the face because I thought he was bringing some religious crap in on me, like, 'you're just my sister in Christ, darlin'.' When I found out he was serious, I hit him again and cried my eyes out for three weeks straight, but after that we were almost like friends. Casual acquaintances, y'know, except that we knew something about each other that hardly anyone else did. But I knew I could never be his sister and he knew he could never be my brother and that was that. I already knew how much Kenny hated Charlie, I just never knew why."*

I wasn't the first one to read into that line about 'he knew, I knew we'd never be brother and sister,' and think, 'damn it all, they were having incestual relations,' and Kenny was out for revenge against the guy who spoiled his sister. But then we got to thinking how she said — and everyone knew — those boys were deep in the throes of animosity long before Sandy was going ga-ga over Charlie. Sure, it all could've been a lie. But then a third party — who claimed no strong ties to either of them — showed up and confirmed Sandy's story by saying Charlie would never hook up with a 15-year-old girl at that time, much less his biological sister.

Why? Because Charlie Fontaine was screwing the mayor, 10 years his senior with a husband and two kids.

How in the world this person found out about the affair was then a mystery, as is why they chose to speak up just then, but the day after that news came out, the source was suddenly impossible to reach and the mayor was gone without a trace.

Needless to say the whole town was in an uproar, and the gossip was spreading like wildfire, as it always does. A murder-suicide in which the victims are connected by a blonde bombshell plucked out of one family and put in the other, plus the mayor's affair with one of them — a significantly younger man — was too good not to be part of a weekly TV drama. But in the city's haste to find their missing mayor and the press's hurry to cover the story, weeks passed before anyone realized that Kenny's younger brother Jeb had also gone missing.

Jeb had been away at college in West Virginia, so no one thought it strange that he hadn't phoned home in a while, until Thanksgiving rolled around and he hadn't called to tell his parents when or if he was coming home. They tracked him down two days later, and soon everybody knew Jeb had been the anonymous third party who phoned in with the information about the affair.

How did he know? He was friends with the mayor's daughter, Angela, who got him a job house-sitting for their family, when they were supposed to be on vacation in Florida for two weeks. But duty calls, and Mama had to come home early on "business" — at which time Jeb Kilbourne happened to be coming over to feed the dogs and caught Charlie and Madam Mayor Benedict locking lips in the living room. The mayor of course paid him more than the prearranged house-sitting wage to keep quiet (raising quite a vicious rumor among us townsfolk about just how much and from what accounts she paid him), but Jeb knew who Charlie was — how much his brother Kenny hated him, and only that he'd broken his sister's heart one day — so he wasn't too fond of the guy. It was only a matter of days before he told Kenny what he had seen, and by then it was less than a month before the shootings occurred.

So, what? Was Kenny sleeping with the mayor too, and wanted her to himself? Had he simply been looking for an excuse to off Charlie, and eventually chose to on the basis of his questionable morality? Or did he act as he thought he should have in the eyes of his younger brother, who knew so little of what happened between Sandy and her "real" brother, in order to carry out justice?

Well, if you're anything like us, the answer — the truth about what happened — was a long shot from what we could've

43

come up with at the time. Exactly one year after the killings, the mayor wrote a letter to her husband from Washington (the state, a long way from here) with all the necessary details of the affair, in an attempt to convince Mr. Benedict that honesty was still the best policy, even though she wanted a divorce (we all got a good laugh at that). But she also added a few words that seemed to be merely included for the sake of our own curiosity as citizens of the Town Which This Tragedy Befell. According to her, Charlie had confided in her his own terror at being discovered, and that he didn't want to leave her but he was also afraid to stay. When she suggested they run away together (this was after the younger Kilbourne witnessed their affair), Charlie didn't see her or answer her calls for weeks. Three days before his murder, Madam Mayor saw Charlie and Kenny having a serious conversation just up the block from Billy's Bar and Barbecue from her car. Charlie appeared to be begging Kenny for something, grabbing his forearm at one point, to which I imagine Kenny responded with a death glare darker than any Charlie had ever seen, and he let go. The desperate look on

Charlie's face must've been too much for the mayor, because she quickly changed the subject of the letter after that.

Jeb was as surprised as the rest of us at this new evidence, but many people were tired of the crime by then, and the deaths of Kenny Kilbourne and Charlie Fontaine were barely a blip on the radar amongst the rumors about our newly installed mayor, and the fate of the old high school, with the paperwork now signed for a new one to be built less than a mile away. The old mayor's family moved away and apparently settled the divorce quietly (not quietly enough to escape our notice, of course), Jeb graduated from the university and is off doing the Peace Corps somewhere (and when asked about his two weeks MIA after the shootings, he said he simply "had to clear his head"), and Sandy is working for Charlie's (her) ma at the travel agency in the city. For most people, the irony of that last part has gone stale, but it still cracks me up a bit.

Whatever happened to the story, though? The scandal? I'll tell you, the tides do change quickly in a small town. To most people, the case of Kenny and Charlie was neatly packaged from the start — the victim and murderer were both dead, and it never seemed like anyone else was involved in the killings. It struck people as strange that Charlie didn't cry out in fear or surprise when Kenny drew the gun, nor did he try to run or hide or draw his own weapon, but whatever the story was, there was no one among the living to worry about. When the people got tired of not getting answers, then got some sort of closure in the ex-mayor's letter, everyone was ready to move on.

Me, I wonder if Charlie didn't ask for it, literally; for whatever reason, maybe out of shame, he'd wanted to off himself and couldn't do it. Just made sense for Kenny to be the one to do him in. Like cats and dogs, some people just seem wired to hate each other. But there are many answers to life's questions, and the mystery surrounding small-town scandals is no exception. Neither is the question of Great Uncle Thythik and his apparent failure at tax evasion. For all we know, the question is the answer, in the sense that it's all we're ever gonna get.

One thing's for sure: The uncertainty makes life a helluva lot more interesting.

# The Voice

I wore a dress to the cemetery today. First time in years I've showed my legs in public, for someone who probably won't even notice. Maybe that's harsh, but so is death.

Then again, maybe I didn't just get a wild hair to get all "dolled up" for Cameron — after all, I never really had before. Maybe it was for me. Of course, I'd started dressing a *little* nicer after we met, but nothing as overt as a light blue sundress in autumn.

Yet there I was, kneeling in the grass by his grave, when his older sister walked up.

"Hi," she said gently, more friendly than I would've expected. "Did you know my brother?"

It hurt to look at her face, a shade of the same fair beauty portrayed in Cameron's, right before me, in the flesh. Thankfully, she just thought I was squinting into the sun, and moved to the other side of the headstone to offer me relief.

I told her yes, I had.

She placed her carefully cut white lilies beside my raggedy wildflowers, and I tried not to think about who knew him best. It wasn't a competition.

"I'm Bethany," she said, offering her hand. I could tell she was nice, not nosy, so I told her my name.

"Nice to meet you Rachel," she said with a smile, and I had to look away. She was older, feminine, but still looked too much like Cameron.

We sat there in silence for a few seconds before she asked that question I have yet to figure out how to truthfully answer:

"How did you know him?"

I could have made up a reason. She didn't know me from Eve; it would've been easy to lie.

Well, for anyone but me. I'm a terrible liar, and anything I might say would almost certainly sound like a lie, and I don't think people like to converse with liars. Unless of course they also are liars, but Bethany didn't seem like one.

So I told her, "It's complicated," which is true. I could feel her staring at me, but I was afraid to make eye contact. I didn't want to see any suspicion there, which is what I expected, because I still feel like a fraud. What *had* I known? Who *had* I fallen in love with?

But I don't think Bethany is a suspicious person, because all she said was, "Well, I hope I'll run into you again." I tried to smile back at her, but it died on my lips as she said, "Tell Cameron 'hi' for me," and walked away.

So I didn't tell her my story. But I'm going to tell you, because I have to tell someone.

We met at Kosciuszko Park in Milwaukee, a stone's throw

away from the cemetery where he's buried. I was in my third year at the university, and I'd made a habit of visiting the park every day after class — mostly to read or otherwise distract myself from the fact that I had no idea what I wanted to do with my life. I only have a little better idea now.

In any case, one afternoon, I was sitting on a bench with my earbuds in — not actually listening to anything, but attempting to block out any potential conversation with anyone — when I heard someone say, "Hello." As you probably know, it's quite bold to strike up a conversation with someone who's clearly tuning out the world around them, and such an action is usually only acceptable in dire circumstances (like some creep is following you or you're bleeding profusely and there's no one else around to help). Barring that, you're going to be assumed some combination of homeless, on drugs, mentally ill, or otherwise inept at processing social cues for such an approach.

So at first, I ignored him, pretending I hadn't heard. Then he tried again.

"Hi," he said.

I looked up, ready to level this guy with my best what-the-hell-do-you-want stare, but no one was there. I pulled out my earbuds and searched all around me. A few joggers were running on the path, and I saw some picnickers a bit beyond that, but otherwise the park was empty. I checked my phone to see if I had accidentally stumbled into some kind of help chat, but I had no apps open, and all means of wireless connection were turned off.

I thought I was hearing things.

*I must be tired*, I thought, *or low on coffee. Or food.* (I didn't think about it before, but it occurs to me now that we're always trying to find explanations for things that can't be explained.) *I'm probably just stressed*, was another thought I had at the time. It was the end of spring semester, and finals were coming up, so I used stress as an excuse for any abnormality or change in my physical or psychological state.

I had just put my earbuds back in when he spoke again; the guy was indefatigable.

"Can you hear me?"

I ripped my earbuds out, my heart pounding. I stood up and looked across the lake, thinking I was in one of those weird spots where you can hear someone across a long distance because of the acoustics — like in Grand Central Station, or on Capitol Hill. (I've never been, but of course I've read about it.) The paranoid part of me also considered that I was the guinea pig of some new, high-tech, top-secret surveillance system some government agency was trying out. Then he spoke again:

"I'll take that as a yes."

His voice wasn't threatening — in fact, it's essentially what made me fall in love with him — but I was determined to find him.

"Where are you?" I asked quietly. I figured he had to be able to hear *me* if I could hear *him* so clearly.

And I was right.

"Hey! You *can* hear me! I really wasn't sure if I was coming through." He sounded genuinely happy to discover this, and a smile was on my lips before I could stop it. I couldn't remember the last time someone had been so elated just to hear me say hello.

"But to answer your question, I'm here, in the park."

It wasn't enough to relieve me, or my curiosity. When I think back on it now, I realize it was actually pretty clever. If Cameron had been standing there in front of me, I probably would've ignored him, or told him to leave me alone, if not in so many words. As much as I'd like to say I'm a strong, independent woman, I generally try to avoid confrontation. But at that moment, I was utterly engaged in the mystery.

"Where?" I asked again. "I don't see you."

"I'm aware," he said, and I swear I could hear an impish smile in his voice. "But that's all part of the fun, don't you think? My name's Cameron."

I don't know what compelled me to play the game, but I did. I told him my name, and then we talked. I sat down, put my earbuds back in, and just acted like I was on a call with someone.

I bet you never considered a person could fall in love with a voice, but I did. It was silky, and when I say silky, I don't mean in a creepy, come-on kind of way, but it was calming, and handsome.

Yes, a voice can be handsome, too — add that to your list of considerations.

Cameron told me he was a teacher, and that he'd grown up in Milwaukee but gone to college in Chicago. I told him I'd grown up in Madison, and that I'd never been to the Windy City.

He was astonished.

"How is that possible?" he asked.

I shrugged, not sure if he could see me as well as hear me from his vantage point. My parents had never been big on travel, and, somewhat ironically, I was usually very hesitant to try new things, much less in crowded places.

In a spasm of vulnerability, I told him this, and he basically asked me out:

"Well, maybe we'll see it together sometime."

My heart leapt into my throat. As thrilled as I was to be flirting with this invisible stranger, I wondered if I'd gone too far. I still didn't know what he looked like, or how old he was.

He seemed to understand my silence and backtracked a little. "Or you could go on your own, with your friends. Promise me you'll go, though, just to say you did. On St. Patrick's Day, when they turn the river green."

How I wish we could've done just that. But we didn't, and now we won't.

I told him I'd think about it, and that I had to get back to my dorm.

"OK, but hang on," he said, as I rose to leave. We'd only been acquainted twenty minutes or so, but his voice already tethered me, and I stopped.

"Give it to me straight," he requested. "Is this totally weirding you out?"

As I said, I'm a bad liar, but I also hate conflict — to include disappointing people I barely know — so I said, "A bit." Cameron sighed. "I figured. Would it help if I promised to make it up to you?"

I scanned the park one more time, looking for a face to put with the voice. Nothing.

"You don't have to promise me anything," I said. "We were just making conversation."

In truth, as nervous as I was, I was also dying to meet him.

"Well," he said, undeterred, "if you're here tomorrow, I will be too."

I smiled and said, "Good to know," feeling empowered as I left. I had never been the one to walk away, but already I was changing.

These days, people don't like to let on that other people change them. But I'm not ashamed to admit it. Cameron had a bold personality, a love for life that sometimes makes me angry. It's still painful to think of his existence cut short, that he won't get to watch his favorite movies and I won't hear him singing our favorite Tears for Fears songs ever again.

But maybe we were never meant to be.

Sitting in my room at my parents' house now, remembering how we met, I'm half-expecting him to speak, to remember with me, or even show up right here, just as I'm willing it to happen.

But I know he won't do that. Not anymore.

Honestly, this is going to sound ridiculous, but for a long time I was too *embarrassed* to ask all the questions you'll probably have reading this. I mean, can you imagine asking a person you just met, via invisible voice communication, if they're even human? I do wonder what would have happened if I had stayed in the park that day, and demanded answers to all those seemingly important questions, like, how can I hear you? Why can't I see you? What *are* you? I wonder if it would've frustrated me, to the point where I simply abandoned him; would I have allowed myself to fall in love?

Of course, it doesn't really matter. I did fall in love with him — I *am* in love with him — and there's nothing anyone can do to change that.

After our first meeting, though, I headed straight back to my dorm room and tried my best to forget about it. I went about my evening routine, studying and making dinner, exchanging pleasantries with the roommate I'd been assigned that fall, whom I had just started to consider a friend. I wasn't about to discuss The Voice with her then, and I still haven't, though she suspects I have a boyfriend.

Boyfriend. What a hopelessly inadequate description of what Cameron is to me.

The next day I returned to the park — as promised, but also just because it was already my habit — and I waited. Despite my observations (or lack thereof) the day before, I couldn't help but scan the area for someone who looked like they might have a voice like Cameron's. Just as my soul was being slightly crushed by the girl sidling up to the hot, sweaty hunk stretching by the water fountain, The Voice came back.

"Hey."

I jumped, and engaged in what amounts to kicking yourself internally, even though probably no one noticed. Except Cameron.

"Sorry, didn't mean to startle you," he said, and I imagined him sitting down next to me, though I didn't actually sense anything. My eyes slid back to the water fountain couple.

"I'm glad you came back," Cameron continued, but I was too preoccupied with Ken and Barbie to respond.

Then they started jogging again, and I was mortified to see them coming my way. I always worry about attractive people sensing my attraction to them from miles away, then confronting me about it, thereby causing me to die of embarrassment.

Can you imagine what it's like having an attractive voice *in your head,* at the same time Hotty McHotterton is heading toward you? My anxiety levels were through the roof.

But Cameron couldn't actually read my mind, and at the time he thought I was ignoring him.

"We can go somewhere else if you like," he said, so kindly I felt guilty. Instead of answering, I busied myself with my phone until the couple passed, then stood up and started walking in the opposite direction of the way I'd left before. I stepped off the path and into the grass, taking care not to venture so far that The Voice might think I was ditching him. Once I thought I was out of earshot of the moms supervising their kids and any runners not wearing earbuds, I dropped my messenger bag at the base of a tree that looked like it might be dry. It wasn't, so I stood up again and flopped open the cover of my bag to sit on it.

"All comfy now?" he asked, and I nodded, still not sure if or how well he could see me. Feeling bold (and a little crazy), I returned to the previous day's pressing question:

"Where are you?"

"I'm right here." I looked around and still couldn't see him, so I had a feeling he just didn't want to tell me. I tried a different angle:

"Can you see me?"

A second passed before he answered me with a question of his own: "Why do you ask?"

That one threw me, and I debated how to answer. Keeping my cards close to my chest, as my dad always tells me to do, I went for a superficial explanation. "I just nodded and you didn't say anything."

He didn't miss a beat. "Was I supposed to say something?"

I couldn't think how to answer. I was starting to get anxious again, and I guess he noticed, because he gave me a real answer.

"You do have nice eyes," he said gently. "They're a really pretty blue."

I hadn't been expecting that. I drew in a breath, and he *laughed*. He laughed, and it was beautiful.

"Are you always so serious?" he asked, and despite being enraptured, I was also annoyed, and I let it show on my face.

"No," I muttered, scrolling through my phone again.

"I'm sorry," he said. "I really was trying to give you a compliment. This isn't easy for me either."

And there it was — that slight bit of uncertainty about himself that won me to him, a kindred spirit.

Maybe it will surprise you, but I don't remember exactly what we talked about after that. And it went that way for the next two days, before I asked why *I* couldn't see *him*.

"You're going to hate this," he said, "I know. But it's complicated."

"So complicated you won't tell me?"

I imagined him biting his lip — one of the first things I imagined about his physical appearance, come to think of it. Even with my great imagination, he was still impossible to picture — until I found out who he really was.

In those days, I still looked up when he went silent, thinking I would be able to read the expression of a person sitting in front of me. It's amazing how invisible those things are to you, in a "normal" relationship, when you have those non-verbal cues to rely on to tell you what a person is thinking. I almost never knew what Cameron was thinking.

"Not yet," is how he answered my question at the time. Back then, it was playful. After a few months, his responses became more...morose. He sounded distant, tired even. I tried to ask him about it, but he would either change the subject or stop talking altogether.

Those were the bad times. But there were oh so many good times.

We did crosswords together. He helped me edit my college papers. Regaled me with tales of his childhood, like running from his sister as she chased him around the house with a baseball bat after he read a love letter she'd written to a crush when she was in high school. We swapped stories of doing stupid things while drunk — him, accidentally lighting off fireworks in his friend's car, me, kicking a picture off the wall in a pub while sitting upside down on a bench at closing time — and he sang for me. He *sang*, and I thought he might be an angel, though of course I had no real experience to compare with it. He encouraged me to write for fun, to create, and to get out of my shell, in more ways than one.

It was about this time last year (during fall break) that I got up the courage to ask (read: *lie to*) my parents for some money to go see The Bean. Of course I told them I was going with my roommate, and I swear to god, they practically shoved those two twenty dollar bills into my hands and pushed me out the door, they were so elated at the thought of me doing *something* with *someone* anywhere outside of our neighborhood, let alone Madison.

That's how much of a shut-in I am — or was — aside from visiting Cameron at the park.

So there I was, on the bus, trying my best to touch as little as possible — including the smelly old man sitting in front of me who kept stretching his arms over the back of the seat and vigorously scratching the long dirty hair on his head. In general, I try not to be judgmental, but I also hate being in unfamiliar places around unfamiliar people. Call me a germaphobe, but at least I won't get lice. I hope.

Anyway, I was trying to distract myself. In my head, I kept running through all the things I might say or do when we would meet, really meet. Of course, I tried to keep myself from expecting too much, since he hadn't actually said he would be there. And, though I hadn't realized it yet, he was beginning to fade.

Fading away. This is the first time I've referred to it like that. I'd be lying if I said it didn't scare me.

At the beginning of that week, he'd given me an address. Sort of. A park on Lake Michigan, which was a lot like the one in Milwaukee, and I told him that, but he insisted.

"Just promise me you'll be there. By the end of the week." Moved by the urgency of his voice, I promised. But in my heart I hadn't, because honestly I was afraid of what I'd find. I tried to tell him the day before when I'd be coming, but I hadn't heard from him since he told me about the park. I tried not to think about what that might mean.

Chicago. What a horrible place it will forever be.

I went to the park, but first I went to The Bean, just to ease my guilty conscience. And of course, check it off my list as one of the many overrated, tourist-y landmarks I'd been berated for

57

not having visited — 'what, you've never seen the Cherry on the Spoon? And you call yourself an American!'

That self-deprecating humor I used to hide my shame and sorrow, which Cameron tried so hard to discourage, still rears its head sometimes. I guess he lost that battle.

When I arrived at the park, the truth hit me, and it still brings tears to my eyes. But standing there, at the edge of the lake at almost-sunset that day, I was frozen. Of all the scenarios I had come up with, for some reason, the reality hadn't been one of them.

Cameron was a real person. Emphasis on *was*.

I read the first two lines of his memorial plaque over and over. "In memory of Cameron Turner, beloved son and teacher." *Whose son?* I thought. *Whose teacher?*

I skipped to the bottom, and my heart fell with it.

## JUNE 1995 – APRIL 2019

Before I could process the death of someone I'd never met, *and* loved, I saw the words below — the second half of the chorus of Jimmy Eat World's "Hear You Me."

Morbid as it may seem, at one point I'd considered this in the running for what might have been "our song." Now, it seems exclusively his.

After that, I just sat down right at the shoreline, afraid to touch it, afraid to move, afraid to think. When it started to get dark, I roused myself in what probably looked like a zombie-like state to trudge to the nearest Starbucks for the free Wi-Fi (because who can afford data?). You might think being around people was the last thing I'd want to do, but sometimes that's exactly where I have to go to be alone. I popped in my earbuds, pulled up a web browser, typed in his name, and with bated breath tapped the link to a news story from a Wisconsin paper: The headline read, "Body of Chicago middle school

58

teacher retrieved from Lake Michigan."

He'd lived there, in Chicago, and was found in Milwaukee. I forced myself to read on, biting back the tears, and learned, true to form, he was a downright saint. Long hours after school planning or hosting a writing club, 4.0 student through college, played on an adult volleyball team that raised money for kids with cancer.

And he drowned in a longboat in Lake Michigan. They found his body on May 2nd.

I guess at the time I was still in shock — too shocked to shed tears. I had to know more, but his obituary almost broke down the dam. I saw his face, for the first time. His blond hair, his soft brown eyes, a cherubic touch to his otherwise masculine face. He was, as I suspected, utterly gorgeous.

But that wasn't the worst part. Or, maybe it was, but there was more that compounded my hurt. The celebration of life had taken place in Madison. His parents lived in Madison. He grew up in Madison.

He was buried in Madison.

I didn't care if my crying made people uncomfortable, in the streets or on the bus. I headed home, then straight to *our* park.

I arrived at almost midnight. I texted my parents to tell them I was staying the night with my roommate, and waited there, alone.

I don't know how I didn't see it before. There's a cemetery, just on the other side of the lake. It's where Cameron is buried.

When I got there, I called his name for what seemed like half an hour. Quietly, at first, but finally I yelled for him. My pain was so loud, I almost didn't hear him respond.

"Rachel."

He sounded exhausted, but I didn't even bother with pleasantries before I laid into him.

"How could you not tell me?"

"I didn't know this would happen," he said, and my mouth dropped open. I threw my hands in the air; I spluttered.

"Know *what* would happen?" I hissed. "You've been dead for *six months!*"

My voice broke on the last words, and I crumbled to the ground. I looked up at the stars to keep the tears from spilling out again.

"That's not — I didn't know I would... I thought maybe I'd be here for a long time."

All I had was my anger. I hadn't stopped to process what Cameron being a ghost actually meant, and how everything fit together.

"What do you mean?" I asked.

That's when he explained the fade, as best he could.

"I think, it's my soul, this voice that talks to you — it's attached to my body, and my body is decomposing." I bit my lip and tried not to throw up. It wasn't revulsion at the idea of rotting flesh, though as I write those words, I don't feel any better. It was revulsion at the possibility that I had been right. He wasn't going to stay with me.

"I think, when it decomposes enough, we'll be separated, and I'll go... wherever people go, after life."

My teeth clenched, but I tried to speak clearly. "Why?"

He was silent, and for a panicked moment I thought he'd left me. Then he asked, "Why do I think that, or why will I leave?"

My tears were flowing again, and the words wouldn't come, so he answered the first question.

"I don't know. I just feel it."

What could I say?

"I'm so sorry, Rachel." My breath caught in my throat. "I love you," he said, and that's when I started sobbing.

It was a long time before I went back to my parents' house.

After Cameron told me his theory, I didn't go to the park for a few days. My parents left for the weekend the next morning, thank god, so I didn't have to explain why I spent more than 24 hours in bed.

Before a week had passed, I got up the courage to visit the cemetery, with flowers. Putting them on his grave seemed so pointless, with the knowledge that he'd be gone soon, if he wasn't already. But I had to see it. And I wore makeup, for the first time all year, in the hopes that he'd notice, wherever he was.

I never spent a Christmas with Cameron, and I feel a little cheated as this one approaches. It's been a year now, since I've heard his voice, and I'm starting to forget, already, what it sounds like.

A week or so after Chicago, I spent almost an entire day (and half the next) looking for reasons I might have been able to hear him, when no one else could. I told Cameron my findings, and occasionally he would ask a question — usually when he'd been quiet for a while and I called for him to see if he was listening — but he had as little idea as I did. He tried to say I was "special," kind of jokingly, but neither of us were in the mood. Not long after that, he was gone.

I miss him terribly. And sometimes I'm still angry, distraught. But I won't let myself regret falling in love with a voice. Some days I even take comfort in the thought that he might be watching over me, whether he is or not.

I can't know what the future holds. I doubt I could let myself into another relationship with a ghost, but I hope that one day, I'll see him. That Cameron and I will, one day, be equals, and if it doesn't all make sense, at least we will have found peace.

Even now, though, I can't help but entertain the idea that there's a way to be with him, to see him, to hear his voice again. And I know it's reckless — dangerous — but it's also morbidly thrilling.

I know what you're thinking. I *should talk to someone*. That *life is worth living*. And I'm not arguing that. I want life. Life with Cameron. And in this plane of existence, that just isn't possible.

So I'm trading it for another one, my last hopeful act. And if this hurts you, I'm sorry. But if I can, I'll be watching over you, too.


Love,
Rachel

# The Birthday Picture

"DON'T SPEND TOO MUCH TIME up there, Philip," his wife calls from below. "We have to be at the church in an hour."

"Won't be long," he says, climbing the ladder. "Just need to find the one picture."

In the attic, Philip flicks a switch and waits a second or two for the overhead bulb to light the room. Having cleaned most of the house in preparation for the move, only a few boxes remain.

He kneels before the white cardboard one with the handles and the word PICTURES scrawled on top in his wife's hurried handwriting, then removes the lid to reveal five leather-bound photo albums of varying thicknesses. As he tries to remove all of them at once, loose photos scatter about the floor and back into the box.

"Ah, Christ," he mutters, setting the books down. He begins to flip over the fallen photos, moved by the associated memories.

Philip spies one of himself and his brother Andrew, taken at Andrew's university graduation ceremony, and smiles. It shows one of the few occasions they have been caught on film, grinning, at the same time. He turns over another, this one more recent. A shot of him and his wife on their honeymoon in Hawaii. It had been so cliché, but they had loved it.

Hearing his wife's reminder not to dawdle in his head, Philip swipes the remaining photos off the floorboards and into the album at the top of the stack without looking at them. A large old print falls again, landing face up. Faces up, really, as it includes several Philip hasn't seen for a very long time. In fact, he had begun to doubt the picture existed.

"You know, things might go more quickly if I help," says Philip's wife, poking her head through the hatch behind him.

He doesn't respond, possibly because he doesn't hear. Either way, he is transfixed by the photo in front of him.

"Philip?"

"Hm?" he answers, without looking up.

His wife climbs the rest of the way into the attic and leans over him.

"Is that you?" she asks, pointing to the boy in the kilt.

Philip smiles but does not take his eyes off the photo.

"Yep." If his wife finds it humorous, she hides it well.

"What was the occasion?" she asks.

"My birthday," he says, almost apologetic.

"Really?" His wife is surprised. "Who are all those people? I hardly recognize any of them."

Philip looks up at her. "How much time did you say we had?"

*∗*

The year is 1928, and Van P. Marlowe is 15 again. As he yanks his burgundy stockings over his just-sprouting leg hair and up to his knees, he can't believe he's wearing a kilt. In fact, Van thinks he is most definitely dressed like a girl, despite his great aunt Winifred's insistence to the contrary. Her encouragement for Van to get in touch with his "Scottish roots" (hers) goes unappreciated as he shoves his feet into the buckled shoes, which are not only hideous, in his opinion, but also uncomfortably "snug." As it has been a full year since the birthday on which Van received the outfit, the shoes cannot be expected to fit the same as they might have on the day of purchase — too bad he assumed he would never have to do so much as try them on.

Great Aunt Winifred calls to him again from the stairwell, and through the inch-wide gap between his bedroom door and its frame, he can hear the polite smile in her voice, along with the threat lurking behind it:

"Hurry now, Vanny. Wouldn't want to keep our friends and relatives waiting!"

"Tell them they can start without me," Van challenges, failing to hide the irritation in his voice as he struggles with the topmost button on his waistcoat.

"Oh, but everyone is anticipating a photograph of you in the traditional attire!" Winifred replies sweetly. In a later era, Van might be reminded of artificially flavored cough syrup.

"Well if it weren't for this blasted *attire*—" the brass button remains unmanageable — "I would already be down there!" Van grumbles. Then, further under his breath, "You can't have

65

it both ways."

Winifred says nothing. Van can picture her frowning, her wrinkled hands on her wide hips. After another moment, she grunts in disapproval, then turns and lumbers back down to the sitting room.

Glad to be left alone in his itchy, woolen misery for just a bit longer, Van seizes the moment to convince himself that no one of special importance — or intent on blackmailing him — will be waiting downstairs, so he might as well endure it. Just for one night.

He shoves the button as hard as he can into the microscopic hole in which it allegedly fits, only to have it pop right off and roll onto the dirty white carpet at his feet. Van picks up the liberated button — unaware of his bare backside showing as he bends down — and examines the damage. He stares at the space between the button and the snapped thread hanging limply where the button used to be, spits out an "ugh" and throws the button back on the floor.

"Stupid jockey outfit," Van mutters in disgust. "Not even Scottish."

He isn't particularly wrong in his statement — Van's great, great grandfather may have been Scottish, causing quite a scandal when he married Great Aunt Winifred's Welsh mother, but for the Marlowes, England was all they'd ever known, and America is the new England.

Van's brother Andrew is passing time in the parlor with 16-year-old Lizzy Langdon, who is repeatedly flattening the skirt of her pale yellow dress and re-fluffing it nervously. As Miss Langdon shifts uncomfortably on the green-striped settee next to the flirtatious boy, adults long past mere legality pay them no heed. Under the guise of socializing, wrinkled hands with age spots and hidden wedding rings pick at finger food with less than honorable intentions. Middle age has done the children's family friends and relatives in, each one now seeking their own escape.

Take Mildred, for example: 40 years old and 90 pounds heavier than when she married almost two decades ago, her pearled neck bulges as she mechanically swallows her fifth deviled egg of the evening; it's been twenty minutes since she arrived at the party.

Then there's Mr. Collier, 57 and sifting through the desperate housewives in the room with a glass of champagne and a rented tuxedo, feigning the kind of wealth that leads astray. Rumors of such wealth instigating fleeting trysts at best and inciting murder at worst come and go every year in the suburbs of New Hampshire.

Ana Potrepalov, in her tight emerald gown, lurks in the corner sipping punch; her deception leaves her past unnoticed. Looking just the part of the seductive mistress, she effortlessly stirs up jealousy in the wives of the men she passes by, leaving more timid women fearfully clutching their husbands' arms. Ana is just the type to attract Mr. Collier's attention — except that he and Mrs. Marlowe alone, in the gaggle of partygoers, already know the secret of her preferences. As it stands, Ana Potrepalov's presence is the only physical evidence of Susan Marlowe's mid-life crisis, which occurred three years earlier.

But Susan is not thinking about that. She's "chatting," as they say, with a quiet couple dressed in pale hues near the door. These are two of her high school friends from Kent, John and Patricia, who have made the journey across the pond for Van's birthday party. Not that Van has so much as met the couple before, but his 15th birthday happens to be the first big event Susan Marlowe has hosted since her husband Lionel's disappearance 21 months ago. John and Patricia are here for moral support, though they do not mention it, and instead regale their old friend with tales from home.

Oblivious to all of this, Andrew continues to pursue Lizzy Langdon, who continues to ignore his pursuits, her thoughts drifting to the boy upstairs, one year her junior. Van is hardly the athletic charmer his brother is, but there was that one time at Hadliegh Park last summer...

*✱*

"What happened at Hadliegh Park?" Philip's wife inquires, her long hair spilling over his shoulder.

He blushes. She raises her eyebrows.

"It was nothing," Philip says hurriedly. "Just a teenage... encounter."

"Really," she says doubtfully, a playful spark in her eye. Philip smiles sheepishly.

*✱*

Van is hesitating at the top of the stairs, listening for signs that the party is going on without him, that the greatest number of attendees are engaged in conversations or pursuits that would draw their attention elsewhere. Satisfied to the highest degree possible in his nervousness, Van takes a deep breath and begins his descent. Three steps from the landing, Van spots the yellow-haired girl on the settee and freezes. His hand goes clammy on the polished railing, and the color drains from his face. The tassels on his cap are still swinging, the instinct to flee overwhelming, but it's too late. Lizzy Langdon looks up and bites her lip to keep from laughing. This does not escape Andrew's attention, as he looks for the cause of his object's sudden change in expression, and locks eyes with his younger brother. There's no stopping the ensuing guffaw.

"Why, you look like a ripe piece of Scottish work, don't you?" Andrew mocks between hoots of laughter. Before Van has a chance to stammer out a comeback that would surely be

flouted by another from his brother, the doorbell rings, and the conversation falls to a quiet mumble. All eyes turn to the door.

"Wonder who that could be..." Van's mother addresses the crowd with a nervous smile as she crosses the room, her taupe heels clacking loudly on the parquet floor. The murmuring picks up, then ceases as Mrs. Marlowe turns the brass knob and opens the door.

"Charles!"

***

"Your *uncle* Charles?" Philip's wife asks, incredulous. She's heard the stories.

"The very same," Philip says wistfully.

*∗*

The party falls silent. Mildred gulps down her mouthful of Cornish pasty, and Mr. Collier chugs his champagne, lunging for another as the server passes. Ana has disappeared to the washroom. Andrew stands up and awkwardly sits back down next to Miss Langdon, who is fidgeting with the hem of her skirt. Van turns his focus to his mother and the man at the door, who is already shouldering his way in. It has been a long time since anyone has seen Uncle Charles.

"Suh-prise!" Uncle Charles booms with all the impropriety of a born-and-bred American, spreading his arms wide. "Didn't think I'd miss one of my own sister's parties, didja?" He grins, already stepping over the threshold with a bottle of cheap wine in hand. Mrs. Marlowe glances down at the label, but Van's eyes are drawn to the missing arm at his uncle's left side. The sleeve of Charles's burgundy dress shirt, rather similar to the shade of Van's stockings, is tied up and pinned neatly where his elbow should be. His brown hair is pomaded and looks as though it has been recently trimmed, but he has not shaved in a day or two. Mrs. Marlowe has a mind to comment, to ask all sorts of questions about what he thinks he is doing here, then notices the phantom limb, and gasps.

She throws a hand to the necklace at her collar. "But Charles! Whatever happened to your arm?"

The room is still silent, save for the tinkling of glasses, the rustling of napkins, and the munching of food, which give the scene an air of melodrama. Charles takes the door from Mrs. Marlowe and closes it behind him. Even from the stairwell, Van can see there is something distant — and, what is it, forlorn? — in his uncle's eyes as he searches for a response. Suddenly, Charles looks up at Van and laughs. Van feels his face get hot, and hotter, as he realizes how red his cheeks must be beneath his sandy brown hair.

"Perhaps that is a story for later, after this young man's been presented!" Charles exclaims, gesturing to Van with the wine bottle. "What's this then, Philip, did old Winifred put you up to this nonsense?"

Van gulps and smiles a little at his uncle's use of his knightlier middle name. He is considering a nod when Great Aunt Winifred steps out from the dining room.

"*Old Winifred* decided it was high time her grand-nephew showed his pride for his country!"

"Oho, *his* country, is it?" Charles challenges, teasing. "Kilts come large enough for English balls now then, hm?" He looks up at Van — who has turned bright red again — with a wide grin, and winks.

Great Aunt Winifred looks as though she is about to explode, spluttering fragments of questions like 'why' and 'how dare you' and 'what nerve,' until finally Mrs. Marlowe steps in and sets a soothing white hand on her aunt's arm. She says to Charles, more than a little late, "Please come in," and takes the wine from him with an insipid smile. Great Aunt Winifred todders off to the kitchen again in a huff.

Mrs. Marlowe hands the bottle to Andrew absently and mutters something about taking it to the table, without looking at him. Instead, she is staring at Charles's missing arm.

Andrew's eyes widen as he snatches the wine from his mother's hand and proudly carries it to the next room, dragging Lizzy with him. She looks up at Van helplessly, and he resists the urge to run after them. Slowly, he continues to descend the stairs.

"Charles..." Mrs. Marlowe begins cautiously, but he is not paying much attention.

"Yes? What?" he says distractedly, picking his teeth. She takes his good arm and walks him into the parlor, where everyone abruptly resumes conversation.

71

"How—" she falters, then asks a question other than the one first on her mind. "How is your sister?"

The conversation in the room falls to a murmur again, a poor disguise of eavesdropping.

"My sister!" Charles says in ill-concealed surprise. "Oh, she's well, I suppose. Been posin' for some magazine in Flor'da or something like that. The other one, well, she's quite a bit too young and pretty to be a divorcée, I'd say, so perhaps she'd make a decent pinup, too." Charles slides Susan a meaningful look and she flushes, fingering her necklace again. A wide, white opal in a blackened silver filigree setting, Van thinks it's an awfully gaudy piece, and his mother knows it is. But as they both know, family takes precedence over fashion.

Van has finally reached the bottom-most step and he practically jumps into the dining room, eager to pursue his brother and the love of his early life. He knows everyone will say it's only a childish crush, but Van knows better. He hopes he can be as smooth as uncle Charles always is.

\*\*\*

Philip's wife is now sitting on the floor of the attic beside him, thus far amused by the tale.

"You mean to tell me you've never thought to breathe a word about your first love?" she says with a smirk.

Philip smiles. Looking meaningfully into her eyes, he says, "It was a strange time."

"I'll say," his wife says, adjusting the neck of her modest black dress. "Why did your mother ask about her own sister that way?"

"She and Charles were step-siblings," Philip explains. "They grew up together, but she and his sister didn't."

His wife puts an arm around his shoulders, a half-smile on her lips. "Who knew your family tree was so convoluted?"

*⁎*

In the dining room, Andrew is pouring the wine.

"Oh Andrew, don't," Lizzy whines quietly. She doesn't want Great Aunt Winifred to overhear — or see — from the kitchen.

"Oh, don't be such a prude, Lizzy," Andrew chides. "Did you see all the liquor everyone brought? They won't miss half a bottle of Uncle Charlie's wine."

Resigned, Lizzy flops down in a wood-backed chair at the table, setting her chin in her hands. When Van enters, she bounces upright and smiles.

Unable to tell if her smile is truly for him or his god-forsaken jockey suit, Van hastily removes his cap and rolls it in his hands. He notices Andrew in his pale yellow tie, just the shade of Lizzy's dress. An intense jealousy moves Van to speak, but his words don't threaten as his thoughts do.

"What're you doing?" he asks, cautiously.

"Well, well, look what the cat coughed up!" Andrew sneers, setting the bottle back in the center of the table.

Lizzy stands abruptly. "I told him not to do it, Van!" she wails.

Andrew makes a sort of *psht* sound. "Aw, what does he care? You want some too, right Vanny?" He holds a glass, half full, up to Van and wiggles his eyebrows, grinning conspiratorially.

Van wrings the cap tighter in his hands, considering his options, shifting his weight from one foot to the other. Andrew rolls his eyes and throws the glass of wine down his gullet,

73

staining his lips a purplish red.

Great Aunt Winifred appears in the doorway to the kitchen, dough stuck to her apron, flour on her neck and hairline. "Now what's all this comm—"

Winifred freezes as her eyes zero in on the empty wine glass, then the opened bottle. Lizzy's delicate hands fly to her lips and Van stops twisting his cap. Andrew hastily sets the glass on the table.

"Well I never!" Winifred storms. "Just what do you think you're doing, young man?"

"I-I—" Andrew begins to stammer, gesturing around him to Lizzy, Van, and anything else in the room that might free him of blame. With everyone staring, he drops his hands to his sides in defeat. "Oh, come on," he starts to plead.

"I'll tell *you* to come on," Winifred says, mildly outraged. "Come on in here away from that wine!"

Andrew's mouth drops open. "What the devil do you expect me to come in there for?"

"To do as I bloody well say, that's what! You can help me finish this pot pie so I can get on with the rest of the meal. And keep your grubby fingers off the alcohol!"

Great Aunt Winifred swivels toward the kitchen and beckons to Andrew with invented urgency. Van imagines hearing Andrew grind his teeth as he glares at him, then slumps into the kitchen. Lizzy looks at Van nervously, unsure of the situation, until Great Aunt Winifred peeks her head out again.

"And don't you two go getting any ideas, either! Off to the parlor, both of you!"

Van turns on his heel and scurries back into the parlor, Lizzy following suit — neither need be told more than once.

In the parlor, Ana has reappeared in a corner of the room, now sipping from an absurdly tall champagne flute. As she looms over Mildred, terrifying her into conversation, she glances at the man standing by the punch bowl. The man is Uncle Charles, who is speaking with Mr. Collier.

"I tell you what, Samuel, you sure know how to dress the part, boy howdy!" Charles hoots, smacking Mr. Collier on the shoulder. Mr. Collier's disdain shows through his smile as he worms his way out from under Charles's grip.

"I'm sure I don't know what you mean," he says tightly. Van notices that Mr. Collier has a rather sharp nose, with a very large forehead. Uncle Charles's face is much softer.

"Oh, I'm not trying to mean anything, Samuel, I'm just saying — you look good! The jewelry business treating you well, hm? Moving up in the ranks, are we?" Uncles Charles reaches across Mr. Collier to snatch a crab cake off the passing platter, then reconsiders. He sets the seafood aside and returns to the punch bowl instead, clumsily ladling the pinkish concoction into a cup resting on the table. Mr. Collier leans back as if he has just smelled something rank, though more likely he does so in fear of being splashed.

"I have always enjoyed my work," he says in vague reply to Charles's question, twisting the ring on his right hand. It is an elaborate gold piece with a pea-sized black stone set into the thick band, the only piece of jewelry he wears besides a large golden wristwatch.

Van wanders over to the settee near the entryway and sits down. His stomach is grumbling.

"What do you suppose they talk about?" Lizzy whispers from behind, resuming her spot on the bench beside the younger Marlowe boy. Van jumps and Lizzy giggles. He reddens and decides not to turn around to reply.

"I don't know. Work, I suppose."

"Oh, but that must be so boring," Lizzy breathes down Van's neck, and he shivers. Suddenly she sits up straight and says, "No, that can't be it. Just look how they laugh and gasp! Surely employment isn't that interesting."

Sure enough, as Van surveys the crowd before him, the whispers and gasps of women huddled in conversation are punctuated by Charles's loud laughter and Mrs. Marlowe's gentle chuckle. Van notices an unfamiliar man seated by the living room window, nervously checking his silver pocket watch and glancing outside. He wears a black sport jacket with gray pinstripes and a matching tie, loose around his limp white collar; he appears to be sweating a little, adjusting his clothing and patting his black hair at frequent intervals.

Lizzy follows Van's gaze. "Who's that?"

The black-haired man looks at Van suddenly, and the boy turns to Lizzy. "I don't know," he says, but if he had thought to say anything further, his words are now lost in Lizzy's wide blue eyes, curiously awaiting some revelation of knowledge. But it doesn't come. Van stares at her blonde curls until she laughs, and he reddens again.

"Van Marlowe, I don't think I've ever seen a boy blush as bad or as often as you!"

Van tries to smile but he is too embarrassed, and it looks more like a grimace. Lizzy laughs again and sets her hand lightly on his arm. "I wouldn't change you for the world."

When it comes time for dinner, the conversation has been exhausted to near utter silence, and the party seems glad to trade the dim, stuffy parlor for the comfort of the dining room. Uncles Charles takes up the rear at a saunter, still talking Mr. Collier's irritable ear off. The black-haired man slips in just ahead of them at the edge of the group, nearest the door. Great Aunt Winifred is hurrying around the table, straightening the napkins and placemats, hissing at Mrs. Marlowe for using the blue ones, not the white ones. But Susan just takes the scolding with a smirk and glides into the kitchen. On her way, she passes Van and lovingly pats him on the cheek. She glances at

Ana and her face hardens, but Van loses the look's significance in Lizzy's laugh as she sits down next to Andrew, who appears rather pleased with himself. Mrs. Marlowe's hand leaves Van's cheek, and the moment is past.

As the guests take their seats, Van trudges to his own at the head of the table. Andrew sniggers again and Lizzy elbows him roughly in the ribs. He stares at her, bewildered, and Van smiles a little, then grins when Lizzy offers him a shy glance. The rest of the party is also silent and fidgeting, until Great Aunt Winifred comes out of the kitchen with an enormous plate of something unidentifiable to Van's "uncultured" palate.

"Here we are," she says proudly. "Homemade haggis!" Great Aunt Winifred sets the steaming pile of sheep guts and stuffing in the center of the table. Mr. Collier rears back from the dish as if it carried the plague. Andrew is white as a sheet now, and Lizzy's cheeks collect a faintly green hue. The black-haired man looks at the haggis somewhat suspiciously, but keeps checking his watch, and Ana stares at the arrangement so intensely that Van wonders if she might be trying to set it ablaze with her sharp green eyes. Mildred's eyes, however, are sparkling with hunger, and Van's water from the smell. Uncle Charles waves his hand in front of his face.

"God almighty Winifred, what the hell is that doin' on the dinner table?"

Winifred's blood boils beneath her cheeks. Van could swear her gray hair stands on end.

"That," she insists, "is a traditional Scottish dish!" Charles guffaws. "Scotland must've produced a boatload of skinny boys and girls then for all the hurling they—"

"Thank you, Charles," a smooth, feminine voice interrupts, before the conflict between Charles and Winifred can escalate further. "But I think that's quite enough."

Mrs. Marlowe has appeared in the kitchen doorway with a large pot pie in her hands and a wan smile on her lips. "Perhaps we can save the haggis for later." A sigh of relief escapes all as she sets the pie on the table and Winifred scurries back and forth from the kitchen, carrying milder dishes: oatcakes and jam, a vat of clam chowder, some mushy green vegetables. The haggis quickly makes its way to the end of the table where Mildred can discreetly claim it for her own.

As emotions cool and food is passed around, poor jokes are made about livestock and lumberyards, and quibbles arise over what's Scottish and what's English or Welsh or whatever else; even the black-haired man offers Van a thin smile, and everyone is once again in good spirits. But Andrew does not allow the elephant in the room to escape inquiry.

"Say, Uncle Charles, what happened to your arm anyway?"

The guests fall silent again and Ana fixes the boy with an angry stare. Andrew wilts under her gaze and looks away. Mrs. Marlowe eyes Charles cautiously and takes another sip of wine, waiting for him to respond.

Seeming to take her look as a signal of encouragement, he answers, "Well, now, that *is* a story." Uncle Charles un-tucks the napkin from his collar and sets it on his half-empty plate. He looks at Ana. "Perhaps Lady Russia would like to tell it."

There is nothing sinister in his question, but a gasp rises from all but Mrs. Marlowe, who simply raises her eyebrows in surprise; the black-haired man, who is apparently immune to family drama; and Ana, who has turned absolutely livid.

"Good *god* Charles, what the hell are you trying to do?" she asks viciously in her thick Russian accent.

Mr. Collier leans over to look at Ana from the opposite corner of the table. "Do? What the bloody hell are you two going on about?"

"Oh shut up Samuel you stupid oaf—"

"Well I say, Miss Potre... Palta..."

"Get on with the story!"

78

"Pass me that cake, will you?"

"I bet she sliced it off, she did!"

"Oh Andrew, why would you say that?"

Van squeezes his eyes shut, his small hands gripping the armrests of his chair, all sound blurring together into a wall of white noise.

"ENOUGH!" Mrs. Marlowe stuns the chaos into silence. Setting her fork down, she glares at Charles impatiently. "Charles, you show up here, unannounced, after two years of no contact whatsoever, with a missing arm and no explanation, and then, then what? You do what you do best, inciting chaos?"

Charles is sheepish, but defensive. "Now, Susan, I don't think that's entirely—"

"No," Susan shoots back. "You do not get to just come into my house and throw all my guests into a tizzy for your own amusement, reminding us all of the disaster of my marriage you so graciously contributed to by advising Lionel to get me a female companion, because you thought it might 'satisfy' me and get me back to 'normal,' then shipping him off to that trollop Daisy, after which I never saw him again!"

**

"Hold on," Philip's wife says, laying a hand on his arm. "Your father left your mother because your uncle told him she was a lesbian?"

He sets the photo down. "I think that's over-simplifying a bit, but yes, my mother... as I said before, was in a bit of a crisis."

"And Charles just assumed he knew the root of the problem?"

Philip opens his mouth to respond but is interrupted by his wife.

"Why, though, would he seek out another woman for your father so quickly?"

Philip frowns. "It's a bit complicated, but Uncle Charles also wasn't the most adept at problem solving. He was never known for having the gentlest touch, either."

***

Charles is speechless. Every other guest (except Mildred, who at some point managed to escape to the kitchen unnoticed, and is now stuffing her face with crème brûlée) stares at their plate in vicariously humiliated horror as Susan Marlowe pants in anger. Finally, she takes a deep breath and says, "Now. What the devil are you doing in my house?"

No one moves, no one speaks for nearly half a minute. Charles sets down his fork, which he now realizes has been hovering millimeters above the place mat, gripped so tightly in his one hand as to put an uncomfortable amount of tension on his arm. He sets his hand down, along with the fork, and looks at his stepsister.

"Susan, I expected you wouldn't deprive me of a visit on my nephew's birthday, and had I known it was invitation only, I— "

"Oh stop it, Charles," Van's mother says, slapping her hand down on the table. "You've never been one to attend family celebrations, you just stick your nose in other people's business and then you leave."

Van has slunk so low in his chair that his chin is nearly even with his plate, not wanting to be the cause of any more discomfort among the guests of his rather unwanted party.

Charles opens his mouth to respond with an accusation to

thwart the insult, then thinks better of it. He turns and smiles at Van, who is trying at all costs not to become a part of the conversation.

"Philip, I'm embarrassed to say I did not bring you a present because I did not remember it being your birthday. In fact, I came to the door, heard the revelry, realized there was a party going on and dashed off to buy a bottle of wine before I rang the bell."

Charles looks at Susan, waiting for her to comment. She says nothing, is only glaring at him, so he returns to his nephew.

"I did not bring you a present, Philip, but I can offer you the story of my missing arm." A rustling is heard as each guest leans forward slightly in his or her chair. "Would you like to hear it?"

Figuring it will take the attention off him, Van nods. "Very good," Charles says, clapping his hand on the table, for lack of another hand. "So here it is."

The guests hold their breath.

"Now I don't want any of you jumping to conclusions, just because I asked Miss Potrepalov to tell the story."

Ana scowls and twists the stem of her wine glass back and forth between her fingers. Despite the misguided reason for her introduction to the Marlowes, she and Susan had become quite close, and she stays in moral support of her friend.

"I'll just tell it straight through, alright?"

Uncle Charles looks around the table and sees Andrew getting impatient.

"Alright," Charles says. He clears his throat. "I was in Florida on leave, six-er-seven months ago, crabbin' with some Army buddies o' mine. We were putzin' out in the flats and we'd caught a few claws but nowhere near our limit. We buzzed back toward shore a little bit until something got caught in the prop and we stopped short. I said, 'What in the blazes was that?' And the boys are all looking over down there and I say, 'hey, ya dumbbells, if we all stand on one side of the boat she's gonna tip.' So they all sit down and I go over there and get my face down by the water to see what I can see. Well, looks like some kelp got all wrapped up in there."

He pauses to glance at Ana. Her jaw is tight, but she says nothing, and he continues.

"So I reach down there —"

"Oh Charles tell me you turned the engine off," Susan interrupts, a mix of concern and chastisement in her voice.

"Now hold on, sis, I said I'd tell the story straight and I mean with no interruptions," Charles says.

Susan crosses her arms and Ana scoots back her chair a smidge, attempting to be discreet. Whoever notices says nothing.

"So like I was saying, I reach down there in the water to try and grab a piece of the thing and see what exactly it is or if it's connected to somethin' we might be draggin'. But when I pull it up, it's synthetic-like, and it's more of a wide chunk of something than a rope of seaweed."

Ana stands abruptly, scraping the legs of her chair against the floor, and fixes Uncle Charles with the most hateful stare she can muster. Only she's blushing a little, Van notices, and the emotions don't mix well.

"Go to hell, Charles," she spits, blood flushing her cheeks.

She snatches her handbag from the corner of the chair, offers a curt goodbye to Van's mother and clacks out of the room and into the parlor.

"Ana..." Susan says, standing, looking to the door.

Ana swings it open and shut without another glance.

"So Ana was the woman Charles brought to your mother?" Philip's wife asks.

Philip nods. "Only that's not why she was embarrassed. Her self-consciousness had much more to do with a particular vanity."

"Oh?"

Philip checks his watch. "Laura…"

"Alright, alright," she says, waving her hands in surrender. "We've still got time. Tell the story."

**\*\***

Susan looks back at Charles, bewildered.

He gives her a look of his own frustration. "Can I tell the goddamn story?"

"Charles, I—" Susan starts, then closes her mouth and sits.

"Alright so I pull this thing up and it's a friggin' wig. I said, 'how the hell does a wig get out in the ocean and end up in our prop?' Well I look out there and I see this person on the south shore with no hair, wearin' a dress, and I can't figure if it's a man or a woman until I hear her screamin' and holdin' her head like she lost it. So I yell out, 'hey, you lost a wig?'

"She sees me and stops wailin', starts searchin' for somethin' and I go, 'it's stuck in our prop, miss! I don't know if you'll want it back!'"

Andrew sniggers and all eyes turn on him, most unsure whether they should shush him or join him. Charles continues, starting to laugh.

"So, huh, finally, she grabs this sunhat she must've had

83

lyin' around and starts comin' towards us, through the water cuz it's so shallow. Well by this time the boys're outta the boat tryin' to catch crabs with the nets nearby, and I'm yankin' on this hunk o' hair in there, and the bald lady's lopin' towards me, trying to run through the water without fallin' down. I finally tear the wig out and the motor's gone dead, so I start rippin' on the cord to make it start. Well right then one of the guys sloshes his catch back onto the boat and washes the wig out with it. And I go, 'ah hell no, I ain't dealin' with that shit again,' so I go for the hair right as the ignition finally catches, only my hand goin' into the water just makes a wave and pushes that wig into the blades and, me being off balance, my arm slips right in with it."

The whole room cringes, various sounds of disgust and pity escaping the partygoers' lips.

"What about the woman?" Winifred asks. "Who was she?"

"Well she's standin' right there and she's screamin' worse than before and I'm seein' nothin' but blood. Meanwhile the boys got me up and out and the gal runs off, I assume, to call an ambulance. I blacked out a bit and woke up in the back of a taxicab with her and she's talkin' to the driver like 'Lionel, what are the odds?'"

Any lightheartedness is gone from the room. Van sits straight up in his chair, Andrew's mouth drops open and their mother's lips are a tight line beneath her wide eyes.

"You mean to say," she begins, then pauses. "Lionel and Ana..."

"Ana!" Winifred and Mr. Collier exclaim in surprise, but they're ignored.

"No-no-no," Charles says, waving a hand. "Lady Russia still swims for the same team, she—"

"What then?" Susan asks, her anxiety mounting. "Lionel has been living with Daisy in Florida and working as a cab-

84

bie?"

Patricia, of the young couple seated beside Mrs. Marlowe, sets a gentle hand on her friend's. Susan stares at her momentarily, fear and confusion in her eyes, but is redirected by Charles's voice.

"No," Charles says slowly, glancing around the table. "He is not with Daisy, or Ana. She was there, I imagine, to tell him what a shit he was and that, despite everything, you two were friends."

Susan looks down at her plate, her eyes glassy.

"And just friends," Charles continues, trying to gauge the veracity of his theory. When his stepsister says nothing, he makes a thinly veiled appeal on behalf of his brother-in-law:

"He saved my life, Susan, and now he wants to come home."

The room is quiet for all of four seconds before the opinions hit.

"Surely you have no intention of letting that man back into your life, Susan," Winifred warns.

"*That man* and I were married for 15 years," Susan says tearfully.

"Yes, but it's in the past."

"Why doesn't he come here himself?"

"What could possibly motivate him to—"

"You know you don't have to decide anything right now, Susan—"

"Don't you think you should at least talk to him?"

"What kind of man—"

"How can you say that?"

The noise is too much for young Van, eyes shut tight, and suddenly, he cannot remain in his own thoughts any longer.

Perhaps, he has some sympathy for his mother, and so decides to create a distraction. Opening his eyes, Van jumps out of his chair and yells the first thing that comes to mind:

"I love you Lizzy Langdon!"

The whole crowd pauses, then bursts into hysterical laughter as Van turns a deep crimson. Lizzy's face runs through myriad emotions as she opens her mouth, covers it with her hands, blushes, and finally, smiles. Mr. Collier is shaking with mirth — as are most of the guests — and draws out a handkerchief to dab at his watery eyes. Everyone is so overcome with inexplicable, giddy laughter that no one notices the black-haired man glance at his watch, mutter "God's blood," followed by something in German, and slip away from the table. Susan is still wiping her eyes with a manicured hand as she catches sight of the black-haired man at the door, and then he is gone.

"Ah, young love," Charles finally says, looking at Van affectionately. "A great occasion for a photo op, hm?"

Charles winks at Van again, now a co-conspirator in his nephew's diversion. Susan smiles at Lizzy in such a motherly fashion that the girl is forced to look away, but still she is happy, beneath her enormous blush.

As if on cue, Winifred has gone to fetch the camera and comes puttering back in with the vitality of someone half her age, a huge smile on her powdered face. "Go stand by the wall, Vanny dear," she croons.

Van hasn't moved since his embarrassing outburst, and as Uncle Charles claps him on the shoulder he jumps back to reality. Charles laughs. "You are your father's son, hm? Bold little devil!" Van smiles awkwardly and lets Uncles Charles lead him to the white-lined wallpaper behind his side of the table. Lizzy comes running to take Van's right arm — he gladly receives her, elated — and Mrs. Marlowe has returned to her characteristically subdued state as she takes up her position on Charles's right, behind Van.

"You too, Andrew, get in the picture in front of Charles, next to Vanny there," Winifred orders, hastily waving the boy over. Andrew wears a mutinous scowl on his face, but Van dismisses it and no one else seems to notice; he could not feel more accomplished than he had at Hadliegh Park last summer, when he had stolen a kiss from Miss Langdon, unobserved. She had since claimed that it was more of a one-time gift than a promise of anything to come, but clearly, and fortuitously enough for Van, she had changed her mind.

Ana and the black-haired man have been forgotten, along with mild-mannered Mildred, who steps out of the kitchen just in time to see Winifred pushing her round bottom against the edge of the dinner table, leaning back with the eyepiece of the camera pressed to her face.

"Everybody say 'haggis'!" Charles says gleefully, once again drawing laughter from the subjects of the portrait as Great Aunt Winifred snaps the photo with a flash. Mildred only manages to move half her girth into the frame in time. Susan Marlowe looks a bit tired, and Andrew is clearly envious of Van, but everyone is smiling, and Winifred is satisfied. Even Mr. Collier is once again in good spirits as he converses with the nondescript couple from Kent.

*\*\**

"Wait," Laura says, as Philip moves to exit the attic. "Who was the black-haired man?"

Philip helps his wife up off the floor and smiles. "My godfather."

Laura's eyes grow wide. "And you didn't know him?" Philip shakes his head. "We had never met. I had heard of him, but it wasn't until later that I put two and two together."

"Oh my, look at the time," Mildred says loudly, to no one in particular, as she heads toward the exit. Uncle Charles and Mrs. Marlowe are speaking more easily, but hushed, and Great Aunt Winifred is fussing over the young lovers, who seem to have forgotten everyone else in the room. The remaining guests pay Mildred no mind.

"I suppose I must be going," she continues desperately. "Reinhard could be home any minute, you know. I've been expecting a letter, but the Post Office could have misplaced it, of course..."

Winifred is now adjusting Van's outfit and Andrew has stalked off to his room upstairs. The party remains unmoved.

"I've had a lovely time!" Mildred calls as she plods dramatically back into the parlor. She picks up her sable mink coat off the bench by the door and peers back into the dining room one last time before exiting the house with a scowl on her face. She heaves herself into the little green bug she drove to the party just hours ago, and rifles through her enormous white purse for the keys. Once they are in the ignition, she begins to weep. Suddenly, there is a tap on the driver's side window. Surprised and ashamed, Mildred hastily wipes her eyes and turns to see none other but the black-haired man.

"Mildred," he says softly. "What are you doing?" With a labored rotation of the window crank, Mildred sends the glass barrier between them down a few inches.

"Oh, Garrick, you know I can't stand social gatherings without Reinhard," she blubbers.

"I know," he says, setting a hand on the roof of the car. He lets her cry for a moment longer, contemplating whether to give her the news. After a time, he says, "I received word from the embassy."

Mildred's breathing slows, her eyes hopeful. Garrick's are not.

"Still no sign of him."

A sob catches in Mildred's throat, but she fights to maintain some composure. A question registers on her face, then escapes her lips:

"How do you do it?"

Garrick gives her a puzzled look.

"Go to parties, when your own brother could be dead?" Her awe turns bitter as she spits the last word.

Garrick's face softens. "Years of practice."

\*\*\*

"So how come I never met any of these friends of your mother's?" Laura asks, snapping her seat belt into the lock.

Philip checks his mirrors as he ponders the question. "I guess they reminded her of harder times," he says, turning out onto the street.

Laura accepts this answer in silence, watching the trees lining their quiet neighborhood meld into concrete towers, swarmed with the sounds of other cars making their way to various destinations.

"Did your mother ever talk to your father again?" she asks. "And did they ever find Mildred's husband?"

Philip answers the second question first. "I'm pretty sure Reinhard's body was located somewhere off the coast of Greece a few months later. Like I said, I didn't know who Garrick was at the time, but he and his brother had apparently served in the military with my father — before Daisy — and became good friends. Reinhard wouldn't have forgiven him for leaving my mom, probably, but Garrick, I guess, has always

89

been neutral when it comes to those kinds of things."

Philip pulls into the lot preceding a plain white church, squarish except for the slopes of the roof and the 20-foot steeple puncturing the pale blue sky. He moves to exit the vehicle, but Laura is still strapped in, waiting for more.

Philip sighs. "And no," he says, staring at the steering wheel. "My parents never did talk again."

Laura gives him a sympathetic look. He offers a half-smile.

As the couple enters the church, they note the empty pews behind a small black mass at the front of the sanctuary, a half-life-size portrait of Susan Marlowe on a pedestal beside her coffin. She wears the opal necklace with the black filigree setting — Winifred's choice, most likely.

Laura gives her husband's hand a squeeze and he takes a deep breath, only now realizing he had stopped moving altogether. Continuing his pilgrimage, Philip keeps his eyes down, until he hears a familiar voice.

"Left the kilt in the closet for this one, hm?"

Philip's eyes snap up to see his Uncle Charles rising from his seat with a familiar schoolboy grin. He wears an all-black suit with a rich man's sheen to it, the left arm no more subtly absent than it had been 25 years ago.

"You must be Charles," Laura says softly, extending a hand. Charles takes it, eyebrows raised in surprise.

"Don't tell me your husband's been spreadin' rumors about his favorite uncle," he says with a wink at Philip.

Philip smirks. "My only uncle, you mean."

"Touché," Charles says with a nod.

Sensing the start of the ceremony, the couple moves ahead to their seats. Casting one glance over his shoulder at the congregation before taking his place in the foremost padded pew, Philip is awed by the faces he sees: his brother Andrew and his wife, seated next to Lizzy Langdon and her husband; Mr. Collier, stealing glances at the middle-aged women in the room; Ana Potrepalov, a short veil over her face; John and Patricia, demure as always; Mildred and Garrick, in-laws bound by the one they've lost. Even Winifred is there, still, dashing away tears as she sets eyes on her great nephew.

Philip smiles back, tears coming to his own eyes, and he remembers the photo in his jacket pocket. Taking it in hand, he leaves his wife in the pew for a moment to lay the memory in his mother's casket. Her body has aged, but her beauty hasn't, he thinks. She looks peaceful.

Philip returns to his wife's side with mixed emotions. Laura takes his arm reassuringly. "Just like old times, hm?" she murmurs, with a nudge to his side.

Philip smiles at his wife. "Just like old times."

FIN

# Acknowledgments

FIRST, I'd like to thank the student editors at *Firethorne* for publishing earlier versions of "In Bloom," "Limbo," and "Sunday" while I was a college student, and Richard Schwantes for laughing out loud while reading "The Birthday Picture" in our fiction class with Baker Lawley. That little bit of validation (plus a plot suggestion from another classmate, Brady Mueller) was enough to keep me working on the story and develop it into what it is today. It is also worth mentioning that earlier versions of "Coming Home," "Fulfillment," and "For All We Know" were first published in the Young Adult, Literary and Mystery volumes of the *America's Emerging Writers: Pacific Region* fiction anthologies by Z Publishing in 2019. Thanks also to Alaska Writers Guild for awarding "Gullfoss" an honorable mention in their 2019 quarterly fiction contest, before I became a board member.

Many thanks also to organizations and outlets like Poetry Parley, Verse-Virtual, Tupelo Press, and the Poets Society of New Hampshire, which have kept me writing and reading in the last year. Thanks to my husband, and the rest of my family, for their continual support (in every way); to Briana Bloom, for her courage and willingness to bring my characters and settings to life for the world to see; to the students who read my work and share theirs with me; to the independent bookstores that keep on keepin' on, pandemic or no; and to Simon, Jamey, and Lynn for helping to promote this work with their words.

To all these and many more, I will be forever grateful.

Thank you.

# About the Author

**Caitlin M.S. Buxbaum** is a writer, teacher and "former" journalist born and raised in Alaska. She has a Master of Arts in Teaching Secondary English from University of Alaska Anchorage and a Bachelor of Arts in Japanese Studies and English with an emphasis in Creative Writing from Gustavus Adolphus College. She wrote more than 600 stories in three years as a reporter for the *Mat-Su Valley Frontiersman* and has had work featured in *Alaska Women Speak*, *The Cabinet of Heed*, *The Daily Drunk*, *The Ekphrastic Review*, and *Verse-Virtual*, among other literary magazines. This is her eighth book from Red Sweater Press.

Follow her on Twitter & Instagram: @caitbuxbaum

# About the Illustrator

**Briana Bloom** obtained a bachelor's degree in Studio Art with a minor in Peace Studies from Gustavus Adolphus College. Her favorite mediums are acrylic and watercolor for painting, and permanent markers for drawing. Briana has had her art shown in multiple gallery openings and won best in show for the 2017 Maple Grove Arts Center Halloween art contest. She lives in Anoka, Minnesota with her two cats.

# About the Publisher

ONCE UPON A TIME, when the author of this book first started to think of herself as a writer, there was a red hooded sweatshirt she wore every day — or at least, near enough to every day, that she would become known for it by her friends.

As middle school wore on, and high school came around the bend, the red sweatshirt — affectionately and more conveniently known as the Red Sweater — made fewer and fewer appearances in public, its cuffs having almost completely separated from the arms. Still, it was too big for its owner — she would never be able to fill it.

And so, it came to rest in storage.

But the sweatshirt wasn't forgotten. It lay safely enshrined in a plastic tote, tucked under old yearbooks and framed photos from years gone by, in a warm, wooden shed.

In its current, more abstract incarnation for Red Sweater Press, the red hooded sweatshirt represents that lingering desire for the past, that holding onto of sentimentality and identity, as well as the cultivation of mystery, and perhaps the sense that somewhere along the line, something dramatic happened.

And the story didn't end there.

These are the ideas behind Red Sweater Press, which reflect the kinds of stories this company aims to publish.

We hope you enjoy everything Red Sweater Press has to offer — now, and for many years to come.

# Books by Caitlin M.S. Buxbaum

*Interstitials*

*Stakes*

*The Compendium of Lost Poems*

*Uneven Lanes*

*Wabi Sabi World: An Artist's Search*

*Ever Unknown, Ever Misunderstood*

*Songs from the Underground*

Like this book? Review it! Go to amzn.to/38DuAI7 to review on Amazon or bit.ly/2rLdxDr to review on Goodreads, or simply tell your friends to check it out! Spread the word however you like, just remember: Be specific, be honest, and be fair.

www.ingramcontent.com/pod-product-compliance
Lightning Source LLC
Chambersburg PA
CBHW030212130726
47898CB00012B/993